CONSTABLE
AT THE
FAIR

A perfect feel-good read from one of
Britain's best-loved authors

NICHOLAS RHEA

Constable Nick Mystery Book 35

Revised edition 2022
Joffe Books, London
www.joffebooks.com

First published in Great Britain in 2010
by Robert Hale Limited

This paperback edition was first published
in Great Britain in 2022

ISBN: 978-1-80405-227-3

1. FAIR DEAL

At lunchtime during one of my first days as the village constable of Aidensfield, I was telephoned by Sergeant Oscar Blaketon. I remember it well because he sounded rather flustered as he instructed me to work a four-hour patrol in Ashfordly, my duty to begin within the hour. It meant rescheduling my other plans but that did not cause undue problems.

The situation was that PC Alwyn Foxton, one of the small town's regular complement of police officers, would have normally undertaken that duty but he had been delayed at Eltering Magistrates' Court where he had gone to give evidence in a case of careless driving. While waiting for his case to be heard, the defendant in a preceding prosecution, who had been charged with 'obtaining money by false pretences' had unexpectedly changed his plea from 'guilty' to 'not guilty'. Not only that, he had brought to the court his own solicitor and a couple of witnesses to support his changed plea. The procedure would now involve a fairly lengthy hearing as the evidence was heard and, as a consequence, Alwyn's return would be delayed, which meant the streets of Ashfordly would temporarily have no police cover. Sergeant Blaketon would never tolerate that and so he told

1

me to patrol the town during Alwyn's unexpected absence. My hours would be fairly short—2 p.m. until 6 p.m. Despite the sense of urgency in Blaketon's voice, there was time for me to arrange a quick lunch at home before leaving. Any additional cover would be worked by other officers.

As it was a Friday in early May and also weekly market-day, my tour of duty would be far from boring due to the influx of market traders along with their stalls, vehicles, customers and tourists. Ashfordly market was always busy so I looked forward to that brief interlude: it would make a welcome change from my own rural duties. Immediately after lunch, therefore, I travelled to Ashfordly on my official motor bike and parked it at the police station where I exchanged my crash helmet for a peaked cap before walking the few hundred yards into the town centre. I was soon exchanging banter with local people, traders and their customers.

That kind of police duty served two purposes—one was to present the uniform as a minor but effective form of crime deterrent, coupled with public reassurance that all was well, and the second was to conduct enquiries into outstanding crimes, however minor they might be. Quite frequently there were undetected local crimes that might be solved due to someone connected with the market overhearing gossip or being offered stolen goods. It was the constant flow of this kind of local intelligence to a handful of dedicated officers that helped keep our rural crime rate far lower than our urban counterparts.

As I went about my pleasant work, however, I heard a familiar voice behind me.

'Now then, Constable Rhea, are you seeking bargains, or just snooping?'

It was Claude Jeremiah Greengrass. With his scruffy dog Alfred at his side he was shuffling among the stalls, probably with a view to trying to find a bargain of his own, or perhaps to sell something he had recently acquired. I halted in front of a bric-a-brac stall as he came along to join the small crowd of potential customers who were chattering as they examined the goods on display, wondering whether anything was a sound investment. Claude did not appear to be carrying a bag of any kind so perhaps he was not shopping, but I must admit I wondered if he was hoping to supply something to the traders or perhaps do a spot of bartering. Even though Claude had a reputation for being something of a rogue and a poacher, he was not a thief and I knew he would not be loitering with intent to steal anything. More than likely he would have spotted a bargain among what really looked like unwanted junk. If so, he would do his best to secure it at the lowest possible price. Having briefly pondered the reason for his presence, I asked, 'More to the question, Claude, what are you doing here?'

The stall appeared to be temporarily unattended by its owner, but that was not unusual in Ashfordly market. Traders who were often people working alone needed breaks from time to time and would simply ask a neighbouring stall-holder to look after things during their brief absence. In this case, but only for the briefest of moments, I wondered if the stall actually belonged to Claude. Had he started a new enterprise to dispose of the mountain of useless junk he had amassed over the years?

Even as I pondered the reason for his presence, a plump, dark-haired woman who was wearing colourful woollen clothes and probably in her early fifties appeared behind the display and smiled at us.

'Sorry I was away,' she smiled. 'When one has to go one has to go.'

'Never mind, luv,' beamed Greengrass. 'The constable here has been keeping a beady eye on things as constables do. Nowt's been nicked.'

'One has to be especially vigilant with Claude hanging around!' I laughed. Whenever we met, we exchanged this kind of banter—I knew he would not take my sarcasm seriously.

'There's no need for that kind of insinuation, Constable Rhea. I am a law-abiding citizen as you know, and I'm minding my own legitimate business.' He smiled at the shoppers who were listening to our exchange. 'And that's more than can be said for you. I mind my business, but you mind other folks'. I call that snooping.'

'I call it crime prevention!'

'So, Maisy'—Claude ignored my final retort and turned to the stall-holder—'got anything interesting for me?'

'Have a good look around, Claude. You're welcome to ferret among the stuff on display,' she invited. 'You never know what you might find.'

'Are you buying or selling?' I asked, wondering if he wanted to turn some of his own oddments into cash. Such oddments are called tofferments in the dialect of the North Riding of Yorkshire.

'Just looking.' He grinned mischievously, picking up an antique inkwell to inspect it. It comprised a heavy solid base about four and a half inches by four inches set on four small corner feet with a solid brass edging. The central part was tough green material that looked rather like enamel and it contained a groove for a pen. There was also a square hole that closely fitted a glass inkwell. It was in position and a very tight fit.

The inkwell had a round hinged cap also fashioned in the green enamel-type material with a brass border while the neck was also of brass. It was a very distinctive item and looked most attractive; it was also in very good condition even though the glassware and cap were a little stained with dried dark ink.

I responded. 'I'm just looking too, Claude, and keeping an eye open. There's always something of interest on these stalls.'

'That inkwell used to belong to Lewis Carrol.' Maisy smiled and turned our attention more closely to the object. 'You know, the chap who wrote *Alice in Wonderland*. He used it in Whitby whenever he went there. He used to walk along the beach a lot and spent time in a lodging-house on the West Cliff. It's got a lot of provenance, has that inkwell. He

4

probably wrote his first article for the *Whitby Gazette* by using ink from it.'

'It's got a fair lot of ink stains, so it must have been used,' muttered Claude. 'I've allus fancied an inkwell on my desk; a proper one and a real pen with a nib, not one of those ballpoints.'

'You're just an old romantic, Claude.'

'Mebbe I am, so have you a pen to go with it, Maisy?'

'Sorry, I haven't, but I'll keep my eyes open for one that's suitable. You'll be back one day, no doubt.'

'You can bet your life on that,' he grinned, fondling the inkwell.

'Well, now's your chance,' I said to Claude. 'A nice inkwell with a lot of history attached to it. A worthwhile purchase, I'd say. And it shouldn't be hard to find a matching pen.'

'How do I know that story's true?' Claude asked Maisy. 'I never knew the *Alice in Wonderland* chap went to Whitby?'

'Well he did; it's in all the local history books. But so far as the inkwell is concerned, you can't check the story, Claude, you'll have to trust me. I was told that on good authority and it's certainly of the right period. And I know it came from Whitby and it's from the actual rooms he used.'

'Mebbe I could say it had been used by William Shakespeare?' beamed Claude. 'There could be a bob or two for me in this, so I'll have it, Maisy. So how much do you want?'

'It is true, Claude, everything I've just told you.'

'Aye, well, I believe you, many wouldn't. How much? That's the important question.'

'For you, Claude, an old and dear friend, two pounds.'

'Two quid for an old inkwell? You must be joking, Maisy, even if it was used by a famous author.'

'Take it or leave it.' She spoke with an air of finality.

'How about a discount then? Me being an old friend?'

'Your old-friend's discount is included in that price, Claude. It's a bargain. It would be a lot more to anyone else. Take it or leave it.'

'I'll leave it then,' he snapped, and turned away.

'Hang on, Claude! Don't be impatient! How about one pound fifteen shillings. Five bob discount for an old friend. My final offer. Think hard about it,' and she turned away to attend to more customers.

'What do you think of it, Constable Rhea?' He passed the inkwell to me. It felt heavy, I noted, and looked impressive. Lots of inkwells were coming onto the market at that time, but most were simple glass creations although there were some made of pot that used to sit in school desks. I recalled our old school caretaker going around all the desks to make sure the inkwells were all full before classes assembled. Now children—and adults—used ballpoints and so inkwells were becoming obsolete. That made them collectable.

As Maisy dealt with her other customers leaving Claude to consider her final offer, I turned the antique over in my hands, then removed the glass well from its socket to find a pad of velvet beneath. On the underside of the base, scratched lightly into the brass, I saw the dates 1854-1871.

My heart missed a beat—the dates were crudely scratched, but they were not new by any means. I didn't think they had been added for effect! I decided to tell Claude what I had found—Maisy was busy with her other customers.

'Claude,' I said, pointing to the dates, 'Lewis Carroll went to Whitby seven times at least, and always stayed at 5 East Terrace, that's one of those big houses near the Royal Hotel, overlooking the abbey and harbour.'

'Oh aye?'

'He went there between 1854 and 1871. He also studied mathematics in Whitby—later he got a first class honours degree in Maths. And his brother got married at Sleights near Whitby—so he's got lots of links with the town.'

'How do you know all this?'

'I used to be a bobby on the beat at Whitby, it was part of my local knowledge. And I went to school there. The house he used—it became an hotel—was always being pointed out to tourists. The dates scratched underneath this inkwell were the same dates that Carroll was there. I'd say that was pretty good evidence—and Maisy didn't mention it. I think she would have done if she'd wanted a better price.'

'Does that mean this really belonged to him?'

'I can't say that, no one can, but it's fairly likely he used it, those dates are accurate. I'd say it has very good provenance.'

'Thanks Constable Rhea, you are a real gentleman.'

He waited patiently until Maisy had concluded her business with the other customers, then called across. 'Maisy, I'll take it, I'm thinking of building up a collection of inkwells used by famous authors, they could be collectable things now that these ball-point pens are all the rage.'

And so Claude handed over his £1.15s. 0d. and stuffed the purchase into his overcoat pocket. With Alfred following obediently, he turned to walk away as Maisy began her sales patter with another customer.

'I don't believe a word of that guff about Lewis Carroll,' he said *sotto voce* as we strolled together for a few yards.

'You could do more research into his visits to Whitby,' I suggested. 'Other supporting evidence might turn up somewhere.'

'Aye, well, I might, if I have time. But I really did want the inkwell. So, thank you for your help. Now in turn for a good favour, I'll do you one.'

'Really?'

'Aye, really. So, Constable, you being an observant sort of chap, have you looked high enough and far enough to see what's on the wall of the town hall?'

I must admit I had not noticed anything unusual and wondered what on earth he was going to do next. At Claude's insistence, however, I stared with keen interest as several bystanders overheard his words and followed the direction of my staring.

It reminded me of that old schoolboy jape where someone stands and looks skywards while pointing fingers towards the heavens. There is nothing in the sky, of course, but the children would do that in a busy street without a word being spoken, then people would stop and do the same. Within minutes, a crowd would gather with everyone staring skywards but not knowing what they sought. As they did so, the children who had instigated the plot would quietly walk away to leave the people standing there and looking for nothing. In my youth it was a good May Gosling joke. A May Gosling was someone who had been subjected to, and who had been tricked by, an April-Fool type of joke on the morning of May 1. Persuading people to stare into the sky was often guaranteed to succeed.

Now, in the middle of Ashfordly market and in police uniform I found myself staring at the walls of the town hall as several bystanders did likewise. I began to wonder if I was a victim of that old trick.

'So what are we supposed to be looking at?' I asked Claude after a few seconds.

'That horse collar,' he said, blinking his eyes rapidly and pointing aloft in the direction of the wall. 'Hanging from that hook at the bottom of the flagpole.'

'Horse collar?'

'Aye, that's what I said, Constable. A horse collar.'

I stared even harder but could not see a horse collar. After all, a horse collar is a rather large object that would be difficult to miss, especially if it was hanging from a flagpole fastened to the wall of a public building.

'You're having me on, Claude!' I began to wonder whether I had been subtly tricked. 'There's no horse collar up there . . . but I can see a horse shoe. How did that get up there? I thought horseshoes hanging outside buildings were to keep witches at bay, or to bring good luck, so I could hardly imagine the town council approving of that kind of thing.'

'Look closer, Constable. That's not a horseshoe, it's a miniature horse collar.'

'A miniature one?' I wondered why anyone would want a miniature horse collar—being the size of a horseshoe, it was

8

far too small for even the tiniest of Shetland ponies, unless, of course, it was designed for a toy horse. But if that was the case, why hang it from the town hall's official flagpole?

As I stared at the object, I realized it was rather too far away for me to see every detail, but, as my eyes became adjusted to the distance and the shadows in that area, I could see it was a miniature model of a horse collar. It was made of leather and was complete with a hame strap and hames for the breast plate. I wished I had my binoculars to get a closer view.

The flagpole was a shortened version and did not stand on the ground. Instead, it was fastened to the town hall's stonework with brackets and its base was higher than the first-floor level. It occupied a place upon a gable end of the building, overlooking the market-place.

At that gable end there was a French window opening onto a small balcony. The town's flag, or perhaps some other significant one, could be flown from the pole on ceremonial occasions while important people could address the crowds from the balcony. But now a miniature horse collar was hanging from the base of the flagpole, apparently secured to the bottom bracket.

In truth, it would have been most difficult to see unless it was pointed out and if Claude had not revealed it to me, I would never have noticed it. He was grinning widely at his successful little ruse so, somewhat naïvely, I asked, 'So, Claude, I have to ask the question—what's a tiny horse collar doing on the flagpole?'

'Hanging there.' He laughed at his own joke and the bystanders now joined in. They had all spotted it now and were pointing and discussing its purpose.

'It looks like a model or a toy, so why is it up there, Claude?' was my next question. 'Is it a joke of some kind? One of your pranks perhaps?'

'Now, Constable, think hard. There's no way a man of my age and size could shin up that wall to hang it right up there, ladder or no ladder. So if you want to know what it's doing there, think on the likelihood it might have been put there officially by the town council. So why would they do that?'

'You tell me!' I retorted.

'Well, I'll say no more, but there's a thought for you to chew over as you patrol this market, fighting crime and snooping on private individuals and their business operations.'

'Obviously you know the answer and equally obviously I, being the new lad on the block, don't know what it's all about. So come on, Claude, put us all out of our misery. Let's hear you air your vast knowledge.'

'You did me a favour with that inkwell, so I am about to return it—I'll tell you summat not many folks know.'

'I'm all ears.'

'It's an old tradition.' Now that he had scored a minor victory over the constabulary before an appreciative audience and also received some valuable information, he was quite content to explain. 'Next Monday the town crier will come along and stand on that balcony to shout "Oyez, oyez, oyez, the collar has been hung. The collar has been hung. God Save the Queen".'

'How do you know that? It's news to me. I think the police would have been notified about an official ceremony. It's not in our diary.'

'Be that as it may, Constable, it's going to happen. That's why that collar is hanging there.'

'Now you are having me on, Claude.'

'I'm not, Constable. Would I do such a thing? Me being such an upright and law-abiding citizen?'

'Yes, you would. You know all about it and you are just poking fun at those of us who don't. Look at these people around us—they're all fascinated as well as me!'

'Yes!' shouted a voice from the background. 'Come on, mister, put us out of our misery!'

'I'm testing the constabulary's knowledge. I allus thought our wonderful policemen had to know everything about the district where they worked; local knowledge it's called. They should know why that collar's been hung there.'

'I agree entirely. But I am new to the area, so I want to know what it's all about. So, are you going to tell me—and these other people who are hanging onto your every word as well. We need answers, Claude.'

'It's summat that's going to upset that man Blaketon and all your mates. From what I've been told, on very good authority I might add, it's an old custom that's been revived by the town council, but I don't think those pen-pushers really know what they've done, they've no idea of the meaning of that miniature horse collar. That's what I reckon.'

'Go on, I'm waiting,' I sighed, as he stretched out the period of uncertainty. 'We're all waiting, Claude. Why would the town council revive an old custom that's going to upset the police?'

'Well, I can't answer for the funny decisions of councillors, but I didn't tell you everything. I missed out some of that Oyez thing. After shouting "Oyez, oyez, oyez, the collar has been hung", the crier adds more.'

'The suspense is killing me, Claude.'

'He shouts "The fair is open".'

'Fair? What fair?'

'The Ashfordly Horse Fair.'

'But we don't have a horse fair!'

'Aye, you're right. We don't, but we used to have one. It was first proclaimed in 1585 but fizzled out after the First World War. That marked the decline of the need for horses, Constable. From that time onwards, horses weren't used as much as they were previously. Cars and charabancs were all the rage, trains were running, horses weren't necessary for military operations and fewer were used on farms and by landowners, so the horse fair and the need for it just faded away. There was no trade in horses any more. I think the last Ashfordly Horse Fair was in 1922 or thereabouts, according to that chap who told me all about it.'

'What chap was that?'

'I don't know his name, a chap I met in a pub at Malton, a chap who knows all about horse-dealing, fairs and such.'

'So what's the point in renewing the old custom of raising the horse collar and declaring the fair open if we don't have a fair any longer? And if we don't need horses like we used to? Did your friend explain that?'

'Well, the week after next—the Monday of that week, the one nearest to May 18—was the traditional date of the horse fair. That's why the collar is up there.'

'So was it just a single day?'

'Single day? Not on your life. It lasted all week, from Monday through to Saturday, and everyone left on the Sunday to go their separate ways.'

'To another horse fair?'

'Aye, more than likely. According to what I've heard, being a chap with his ear to the ground so to speak, some crackpot on the council thought it was a good idea to re-enact the old tradition of hoisting the shoe and having that declaration read out again. Keeping the old customs alive, that sort of thing. That's why the horse collar has reappeared up there, according to my mate.'

'Well, I can see no harm in that,' I admitted.

'Suppose I told you that by hoisting that shoe and reading out the proclamation it means that all horse traders who come to the town for that week are exempt from the law for the whole of that week.'

'It was a long time ago, Claude, it couldn't happen now.'

'Aye, I know, but that's the tradition and it continued until the Ashfordly Horse Fair ceased. But suppose all the horse traders come back now that the custom has been revived. And expect to be free from the law. There has been a revival of interest in horses—little girls ride them, they're a part of agricultural shows, hunting, racing and show jumping . . . horses are suddenly big news all over again, Constable. You've even got 'em in the force, police horses. And I might even get myself one or two.'

'I can't see that that kind of activity would require a horse fair, Claude. Those old fairs were patronized by gypsies and travellers.'

'Right, that's it. So just you suppose all those horse traders like you mention, the ones who go to Appleby Horse Fair, Boroughbridge, Stow-on-the-Wold, Barnet, Brampton, Belton and all the others, suppose they now decide to return to Ashfordly?'

'It would make us very busy.'

'Busy? It would be more than that! They don't have to obey any laws or pay the car-parking charges, and they leave muck and litter all over the place, not to say anything about nicking from shops and farms. Now that's summat for the constabulary to think about.'

'They wouldn't do that!'

'They would, Constable, and if my famous ear-to-the-ground technique of keeping touch with country life is concerned, I did hear on the proverbial grapevine that that's exactly what they are going to do! I'm telling you because you just did me a favour. Take it or leave it. But if they do come back to Ashfordly to renew the old horse fair, our quiet little town will be full of travellers and gypsies, ponies and horses and horse-drawn caravans and carts. There'll be horse muck by the ton, all over the place. Just think of all that messy stinking horse muck, Constable. And travelling people aren't all that particular about where they dump their own rubbish and muck.'

'Are you sure about this? That they'll all come to Ashfordly? All because of that horse collar up there?'

'Sure as eggs is eggs, Constable. Telling you in advance is my good deed for the day, my way of thanking you for your help with my inkwell. I could have waited and said nowt, then you and your mates would have been caught by surprise. Mind, it would have been great fun, seeing how Blaketon would have coped!'

'So how many people are we thinking of? And how many horses?'

'Who knows? Hundreds or even thousands of horses, men, women, children along with their caravans, trailers, carts, dogs and even goats. If you'd take my advice, based on years of country knowledge, I reckon it'd be a good idea to have words with your mates in Appleby to see how they cope.'

'We'll have to stop them coming here.'

'You can't do that; it's a free country and the fair was established by charter. You can't get rid of it. Those folks are going to come, believe me. They'll already know about that collar and will regard it as an open invitation.'

'If this is true . . .'

'It's true all right, Constable. I really mean it. I'm not joking; I'm not trying to set you up. You're a decent young copper, you helped me with that inkwell and it's not often coppers help me. They're usually after my blood for summat or other.'

'There's good in everyone, Claude. Even you.'

'I have a heart of gold, Constable Rhea. So there you are, some good realistic intelligence from one who knows. You can't stop 'em coming, so you'll have to cope with 'em. It's as simple as that. But thanks to me, you've got some advance warning.'

My heart sank. How on earth could a small town like Ashfordly cope with thousands of horses and their owners? I had to speak to Sergeant Blaketon without delay. I thanked Claude who went off chuckling to himself about the dilemma we would now have to confront, but first I decided I should try to clarify the true position with someone in the town hall. I was acutely aware that Claude could be having a bit of fun at the expense of the police. It meant I needed to know exactly what lay behind the custom of hoisting the horse collar, but, more importantly, I had to know what plans, if any, the council had made to cope with the anticipated influx of horses and people.

I entered the town hall's mighty portals wondering how long it would take me to track down the person who dealt with miniature horse collars that were hoisted on council flagpoles. When dealing with local authorities, it was always extremely difficult to find the right person who dealt with any given subject. But I had to try. Once inside the main entrance there was a spacious hallway with a beautiful tiled floor and a massive staircase rising to the first floor and beyond.

Around the hall were several ground-floor offices the doors of which were firmly closed, but tucked in a corner on the right, almost behind the main door, was a small cubicle marked 'Rents, Rates and Miscellaneous Payments'. Attached to the payment window, behind which sat a bespectacled woman, was a notice announcing *Enquiries*. I considered that to be a very good start.

As I made my way to Enquiries I saw a large notice-board on the wall adjoining the cubicle. It bore names with arrows pointing to offices both on the ground floor and upstairs. I halted to read the notices. I was soon reading the signs indicating the Town Clerk's Department, Engineers and Surveyors, Public Health, Finance, Housing, Planning Department, Rent, Rates and Valuation, with others too. There were some small-print signs showing that each department contained sub-departments such as museums, septic tank clearance, pest control, conservation, contracts, street collections, hackney carriage licensing, public conveniences, street lighting, footpaths and bridle-ways, electoral registration and many more.

The office of the Registrar of Births, Deaths and Marriages was also in the building as was the street-naming department, but I saw nothing to indicate a department that dealt with flagpoles. The woman in the Rent, Rates and Miscellaneous Payments cubicle realized I had no idea where I wanted to be, so she called out, 'Constable, can I help?'

'I'm looking for the department that deals with flagpoles.'

'Flagpoles? What aspect of flagpoles? Do you wish to erect one on a public building, change the height of the one on the police station, paint yours a different colour, or make a formal complaint about the wrong flags being hoisted in specific areas? Some people do fly them higher than they should, you know, and others are liable to display inappropriate flags, or those that infuriate their neighbours. Or perhaps you wish to fly a particularly symbolic flag on a special day? Sir Robert Peel's birthday perhaps?'

'I had no idea there was so much to know about flag-poles and flags.'

'As the person in charge of enquiries, I have to deal with all manner of odd questions and complaints. So how can I help you with your flagpole?'

'It's not about the one on the police station, it concerns the flagpole outside this building, the one on the wall over-looking the market-place near the balcony. A miniature horse collar has been attached to it, and I'd like to chat to the person who put it there.'

'You mean the person who put the pole up there, or the one who put the horse collar up there?'

'The horse collar.'

'Ah, well, we don't have a special department for flag-poles although we do have one for street lights, another for road signs and one for windmills. However, I am sure Engineers and Surveyors would have installed the pole in the first place. Planning would have given permission for it to be there; Maintenance and Repairs would have painted it and repainted it over the years, and the hoisting of flags on particular dates is the responsibility of the Town Clerk's Department. I am sure our flagpole complies with all the necessary rules and regulations, Constable, but I am afraid I know nothing about the hoisting of horse collars. However, I think you need to talk to Mr Clarence Dennison, he is our Flagpole Liaison Officer. He knows everything there is to know about flagpoles, not merely the official one on this town hall but all sorts of flagpoles and flags. Shall I call him for you?'

'Thank you, yes.'

'Please take a seat,' and she pointed to a bench beside her cubicle.

After a few minutes, a very tall, thin man descended the spectacular staircase. In his middle forties with a neat head of black hair, he was clad in a smart dark suit with a white shirt and blue tie. He strode towards me like a man on stilts and I realized why he had been allocated the important duty of Flagpole Liaison Officer. Clearly, he was built for the job.

'Ah, Constable.' He extended his hand for me to shake. It was like rattling the ropes used to hoist flags. 'Dennison is the name.'

'PC Rhea from Aidensfield.'

'Come into the interview room,' and he led the way, opening one of the unmarked heavy doors, and I found myself in a splendidly furnished room with a conference table, chairs and jugs of water.

'Sit down, PC Rhea. A glass of water perhaps?'

'No thanks, I'm fine.'

'So how can I help you?'

'It concerns the flagpole on the wall of this building near the balcony that overlooks the market-place.'

'Ah yes, very historic it is too. It was erected to mark the official opening of this building by Lord Ashfordly in 1834. That is the original pole, Mr Rhea; its continuing presence is a tribute to the council's care and attention to it and, of course, to the timber from which it is made. Oak, no less. Is there a problem? Has one of the brackets worked loose perhaps? Or has a crack appeared in the woodwork? Has it become a public danger?'

'No, nothing like that. But there is a miniature horse collar attached to the bottom bracket. I am trying to trace the person who placed it there. My information is that it was attached by a member of the town council.'

'Miniature horse collar? Are you sure?'

'It's either that or a horseshoe. I am making enquiries to ascertain how it came to be there, and whether anyone in the council is prepared to explain it to me.'

'This is pretty serious stuff, Constable. I must admit I am totally at a loss about this, I was unaware of such a problem. Please show me.'

I led him outside and pointed to the object in question. He studied it from below but decided it was too high from the ground to view clearly. He asked the woman in the enquiry kiosk to summon the caretaker. In due course, a stocky individual in overalls arrived with an extending ladder over his shoulder. I wondered why they did not use the balcony.

Maybe it was restricted to very special occasions? I guessed the key to the French windows leading onto the balcony would be available only upon filling in a form in triplicate and then obtaining consent from the mayor. It was easier to use a ladder.

'Up there, Mr Lark,' said Mr Dennison, indicating the problem to the caretaker. 'Have a look at it and providing it's safe to detach it, bring it down here.'

As Lark ascended, Mr Dennison told me he had not authorized anyone to attach any kind of object to the official flagpole, assuring me that if anyone had wanted to do such a thing, then he would have been notified. As the council's Flagpole Liaison Officer, he was the only person who could arrange the necessary approval or otherwise. He stressed that no one could touch the flagpole without his permission or knowledge.

When Mr Lark reached the pole, he looked at the object closely then reached out to lift it from the bracket that supported it.

'It is a miniature horse collar, Mr Dennison. Very beautifully crafted if I may say so, complete in every detail. But what's it doing up here? It wasn't there last week.'

'That's what we are trying to establish, Mr Lark. Who put it there, when and why. Fetch it down please!'

Once on *terra firma*, Mr Lark handed the trophy over to Dennison who examined it in some detail, then shook his head. Mr Lark then went away with his ladder, leaving us to discuss the matter. We returned to the conference room away from the gaze of curious bystanders.

'I've never seen this before, Mr Rhea. Here, you have a look.'

There was no doubt it was an exquisitely crafted miniature of a horse collar, a skilled replica of the genuine article that might be worn by a heavy horse. It was in leather too, with metal attachments, a wonderful piece of handiwork and, in my limited opinion, it was of a considerable age. Certainly it had the appearance of being exposed to the weather over a considerable period but it had survived intact. Truly, it was a genuine example of the craftsman's art.

'I just don't understand this, Mr Rhea but I can assure you that it was not placed up there by a council official, I would have known, so I can state quite categorically that it is not an official addition or formal ornamentation of our flagpole. In short, I know nothing about it. So why would anyone hoist that kind of thing on our flagpole? It must have been put there in secret, under cover of darkness perhaps? So, is it some kind of joke? Do you have any theories about it?'

I then told him about the Ashfordly Horse Fair and how, in the past, it had been started by the display of the miniature horse collar followed by the town crier reading a proclamation from the balcony.

'I thought this action might be a devious attempt to revive the horse fair,' I told him. 'I wondered whether some-one within the council had decided to revive it as a form of tourist attraction. You know the sort of thing. You'd have the town crier do his bit and then the proclamation would be read out to welcome and officially open the horse fair. A spot of olde-worlde fun in rural Ashfordly.'

'We don't have a town crier, PC Rhea, and so far as I am aware, the town has never had one. And I doubt if the council would approve the resurrection of a bygone horse fair, not in modern times, but yes, I can confirm there used to be an annual horse fair in Ashfordly and it attracted thousands. But I doubt if it would be welcome nowadays because a big influx of travelling people and their horses would persuade visitors to stay away! And we are trying to attract visitors to Ashfordly,' he said. 'I can say, however, that no such proposal has been aired in our council meetings, certainly not within my time working here—and that is more than fifteen years. Historic though the fair might be, just consider the problems it would create if it was revived; imagine coping with all those people and horses with our limited facilities. So, Mr Rhea, bearing in mind my doubts about the authenticity of that horse collar and its dubious links with the town crier, I suspect this is a joke of some kind.'

'It does make me wonder whether the person who put it there had any idea of the significance of that tiny collar.' As I spoke those words, something occurred to me. 'So what happened to the original collar when the horse fair ceased? Was it kept somewhere? Did someone take it away because there was no further use for it? Could this be that same collar?'

'But I do not know of such a custom, PC Rhea; I doubt if a horse collar was ever used for that purpose.'

'But perhaps there was such a custom many, many years ago. Could someone have found this collar among a deceased relation's belongings and restored it quietly to its rightful place?' I suggested.

'If so, why do it so secretly?'

'Because the person was not supposed to have it! It might have been nicked from the council after the last horse fair was held.'

'That would make sense, Mr Rhea. Way back at that time, a council worker might have thought it was a nice piece of handicraft, or a valuable antique and, because it had no further use, it might have been earmarked for official destruction. That could explain why someone could have taken it home as a sort of souvenir.'

'It happens, Mr Dennison, all too frequently.'

'And now, someone's been going through that person's belongings, perhaps after his or her death, recognized the collar and, knowing its history, decided to replace it, in secret. So yes, I do think that is feasible.'

'Another suggestion is that someone does genuinely feel that the old horse fair should be revived, and this was one way of achieving it. Perhaps that person was seeking some kind of publicity? There's bound to be some old lore within the ranks of travellers and gypsies—if one of them chanced to see the thing up there on the flagpole, they would react, I'm sure. So the old horse collar could have some symbolism,' I put to him.

'Well, yes, word of its presence would quickly spread among the travelling fraternity and they'd see it as an invitation to return here at the appointed time as their forebears had done all those years ago.'

'It is a fact that old traditions are being revived all over the country.'

'They are, and in this case the horse dealers would want to listen to the declaration of freedom of Ashfordly, if only for the duration of the fair. They'd come in their hundreds and thousands with their horses and caravans . . .'

'And they would be exempt from the law?' I reminded him.

'I think we would have to look very carefully into that ancient custom; maybe they were exempt only from certain laws. But according to what you have been told, this is almost certainly the original and genuine collar, Mr Rhea. I can't honestly believe that something so well constructed, and with such an aura of age, would be a duplicate or a replica. Clearly someone has had possession of the original and has decided to make use of it. Or return it secretly to its rightful home.'

'I can't argue with that logic, Mr Dennison. So, can I make a suggestion?'

'Please do.'

'I don't think this discovery should be publicized. If news of this gets into the papers it would certainly create something of a storm and could result in requests for the revival of the horse fair—I think we can all do without that.'

'So what can we do legally? In case the person who put it there suddenly emerges from cover and decides to ask what has happened to it?'

'I ought to say that Claude Jeremiah Greengrass of Aidensfield drew my attention to the collar, and he knows the reason for its presence. He recalls the folklore and tradition behind it.'

'I suppose he mixes with the sort of people to know these things. I might add that we do know Mr Greengrass in our official capacity.'

'So do we! He told me about the message conveyed by the collar and seems to think the travellers and gypsies will have seen it and will take it as an open invitation to return to Ashfordly for a full-scale horse fair, even after an absence of many years. They could be on the way now.'

'Hmm.' I could see his council-trained mind beginning to operate. 'There is one important point, Mr Rhea: I am sure the fair could not proceed without the declaration being read out to them. Displaying the collar alone would not be sufficient, it is the declaration that matters. That is the official bit. But, as I said, I've no idea how that would be done—we don't have a town crier.'

'There must be some records in your files?'

'I'll dig out those old records of the fair to see who and what was involved. They'll be in our loft. And I might just discover who, among the members of our staff at that time, might have got their hands on that collar. Of course, that's if the custom was actually undertaken.'

'Good, then we might have some idea who put it on your flagpole.'

'Right, Mr Rhea. I think we have agreed upon a suitable course of action and I will keep you informed. But can I claim legal custody of this collar? It is ours, isn't it?'

'I'll enter it in the found property register at Ashfordly Police Station. It will say that you found it outside the town hall and that you retained it. If you retain the collar for six months and it is not claimed within that time, it becomes council property. On the other hand, if the collar is claimed by someone else within that time, then it must restored to a genuine loser. If it is not claimed, the town clerk, in his infinite wisdom, might decide to donate it to a local museum, with its full history. That way, the Ashfordly Horse Fair will not be forgotten.'

'I think we can safely deal with this matter, PC Rhea.'

Upon leaving the town hall I returned to the police station in Ashfordly to make the necessary entry in the found property register. As I was completing it, Sergeant Blaketon walked in.

'Ah, Rhea,' he said. 'All quiet?'

'Almost,' I told him. 'I'm just entering an item of found property, a miniature horse collar that was hanging from the town hall flagpole.'

'Is this a joke or something?'

'No, Sergeant,' and I launched into an explanation of the tale, with due mention of the role played by Claude Jeremiah Greengrass.

'Are you telling me that we are to be invaded by the massed ranks of travellers, gypsies, horses and caravans? They can't park on our market-place, Rhea, and we've nowhere else that can accommodate them. They can't gain access to the castle grounds and I doubt if Lord Ashfordly will allow them to park beside the river on his estate. And everyone who leaves his horse or van on our streets will get a parking ticket.'

'I think, Sergeant, you'll have trouble enforcing that. They're all of no fixed abode and they're probably all called Smith.'

'Don't I know it . . . so can we be certain they're coming here?'

'No, we can't. It depends whether any of them saw the collar hanging from the flagpole and passed the word around that the welcoming burghers of Ashfordly are waiting for them. Those travellers have got a very good internal broadcasting system—'

'Leave it with me, Rhea. I've a friend over at Appleby and he keeps in touch with their movements around the country. Next Monday you say? That's when they're due if they really are coming here? It gives us a few days to make the necessary arrangements to get them halted.'

'Right, Sergeant.'

The rest of that day passed quietly and I booked off duty at six to drive home and enjoy tea with my wife and children.

During the following days there was no news of processions of horses and their caravans heading for Ashfordly and by Sunday we were confident that they had not decided to restore the horse fair. Not this year, anyway!

However, I did receive a phone call from Mr Dennison at the town hall. He told me, 'You were right about the Ashfordly Horse Fair, PC Rhea. It used to be held every May beginning on the Monday nearest to the eighteenth, and it lasted until the Saturday following, with the travellers dispersing on Sunday. But it was not in the town centre; it was within Lord Ashfordly's estate, on land near the river. There was an ancient charter that said it must use that land, but it ceased in 1922, through a lack of interest mainly. However, council records contain no references whatever to the custom of the horse collar. And we have never had a town crier. So I think that part of your tale is pure fiction—invented by someone with a good imagination.'

I thanked him for his research, then on the Sunday before the supposed event, I chanced to meet Claude Jeremiah Greengrass as he was leaving the Hopbind Inn at Elsinby. I thought he looked a bit sheepish; his eyes blinked rapidly as I greeted him and blinked even faster when I mentioned the miniature horse collar. In view of what Mr Dennison had told me I decided to tackle him head on!

'That was quite a tale about the horse collar, Claude. Clearly you knew a lot about the history of the horse fair and the legendary role of that wonderful little horse collar . . . so how did you get the collar onto that flagpole?'

He paused and blinked for a long time, then said, 'I meant no harm, Constable Rhea. Just a bit of fun. Really, I wanted rid of that collar; it's been bothering me all these years, after I bought it from the chap who used to work for the council. He told me all about its links with the horse fair but I didn't think he should have had it, or sold it to me, so I didn't sell it on . . . I kept it hidden.'

'Really? So the story is true? About the collar being used to start the horse fair?'

'Yes, well, I thought it was. That's what the chap told me.'

'He might have been kidding, Claude.'

'So how was I to know that? I thought it was real. It sounded real, so I thought that if I took it to a museum they'd ask all sorts of awkward questions, so after hiding it all these years, I reckoned the best thing was to put it back where it belonged. Honestly, I thought it was supposed to hang on the flagpole to start off the horse fair! I wanted to get rid of it; I didn't want it in the house. No harm in that, is there?'

'None at all.'

'Well, I didn't want to get nicked, so I asked a window cleaner to hang it on that pole. He does the town hall windows, you see, early in the morning. I slipped him a quid to do the job.'

'You told a very convincing yarn about the revival of the horse fair though.'

'It was only what I was told, Constable Rhea. I believed every word.'

'It's quite a yarn, Claude,' and I explained how the collar was now being dealt with. I told him that Mr Dennison had contacted me to say he had searched his files, but they contained no record of the collar or its disposal. In fact, he added that there had been no town crier during the 1920s, so the tale about the proclamation was also false. It seemed the entire story of the collar's role with the horse fair might have been a work of fiction even if Claude believed it.

However, because there was no record of an original theft, I assured Claude he would not get into trouble. There was no question of a prosecution for handling stolen goods and I would maintain the secret of his genuine concern. It now seemed that no one knew where the collar had come from, or its history. I explained that the collar, whatever its true story, would now find its way into a museum in a very legal and dignified manner.

The following Monday, however, I was patrolling my patch at Briggsby, only a mile or two out of Ashfordly, when

I saw a procession of three horse-drawn caravans laden with men, women and children and with several piebald horses with dogs and goats trotting behind.

The leader stopped. 'Ashfordly this way, is it, Constable?'

'You're coming for the horse fair, are you?'

'Aye; years ago my family all came here . . . it was held in Lord Ashfordly's grounds, my grandad said. It's nice it's being renewed.'

'Straight ahead.' I then rushed off to warn Sergeant Blaketon.

2. A FAIR COP

One of the highlights of the year in Crampton, a village on my patch, was the annual Mop Fair followed by the Grand Mop Fair Ball. In bygone times, the fair had been held in a field belonging to a previous Lord Crampton of Crampton Hall, but when I was the local constable, the Mop Fair was still functioning and indeed thriving, albeit having been transferred to the green in front of the village hall. The village green had formerly been a level field within the boundaries of Crampton Estate and was located very close to the road through the village. That field had been the site of the original Mop Fair.

In the fairly recent past, however, the field had been donated to the village by one of his lordships. That meant the community benefitted from a place of their own to meet and socialize, both indoors and out, without the inconvenience of constantly seeking permission from the occupants of the hall. It also meant that Lord and Lady Crampton did not have to place their own home and grounds at the disposal of the village when communal events took place, thus ensuring greater privacy for their family.

The villagers of Crampton were rightfully proud of their community hall and made very good use of it. When the hall was completed on that same piece of land in 1894, it was formally opened by the then Lord Crampton. Down the years the Cramptons had shown a keen interest in village life and supported all the local events. They could be relied upon to make speeches, present trophies, and act as judges of things like the best fruitcake or pork pie, the finest six tomatoes on one stem, the longest cucumber, the biggest onion or the heaviest pig. It must have been a hard and trying life, being a member of the aristocracy in a rural setting.

It was against that background that the organizing committee decided that the modern mop fairs with their tents and stalls should take place on the green with further displays inside the village hall. The building would be cleared in good time to accommodate the annual ball and buffet supper during the evening. The Mop Fair brought together the entire village with everyone working hard to make the day a huge success.

When I arrived in the area as the local constable I had no idea what constituted a mop fair. I had a vision of lots of rustic women and girls brandishing mops while going about some ancient fertility rite, or even doing nothing more exciting than selling the mops they had made. I couldn't imagine a fair selling nothing but mops, although when I discovered the origin and purpose of those fairs, I realized they did have strong links with the feminine side of domestic life.

Mop fairs had developed from the hiring fairs that were sometimes known as statute fairs. In some parts of Yorkshire, they were called statis fairs, a local pronunciation of 'statutes'. The people who worked in farms and large estates as labourers or servants were employed for fifty-one weeks out of every year and most lived at their places of work with beds and food provided. Manors and larger farmhouses had separate bedrooms for their staff, inevitably with a second staircase for their use. When each period of fifty-one weeks was complete they had a week's holiday during which time they could go home to see their families, but during that time they were also supposed to find work for the next fifty-one weeks. They did this by attending the hiring fairs that were visited by people wanting staff as well as those who were seeking employment.

The fairs were held in every market-town and also in many larger villages in England and Wales during the week that embraced 11 November. This was the feast day of St Martin of Tours, consequently the hiring fairs became known as the Martinmas Hirings, Martinmas Fairs or simply Hiring Fairs. The hiring fairs became known as statute fairs after they were regulated by law rather than following ancient custom.

Mop fairs can be dated to the middle of the fourteenth century when there was an acute shortage of labour due to the aftermath of the Black Death. A law of the time required every able-bodied man to offer himself for hire at a fixed rate of payment, then an Act of 1563 confirmed, strengthened and extended that law. The decline of hiring fairs began in the 1860s when Servants' Registration Offices were established and the end came with the establishment of Labour Exchanges in 1909.

Surprisingly, memories of the old hiring fairs in rural areas prevailed well into the twentieth century and even later. In fact, some continued for several years after 1909 but they were probably unofficial and perhaps illegal.

When attending the hiring fairs, hopeful workers would have to present themselves to prospective employers who would question them and test their strength or skills before appointing them. It became traditional for the workers, male and female, to carry a particular object that would indicate to an observer the type of work they were prepared to undertake. For example, milkmaids would wear a tuft of cow's hair, shepherds placed a lock of sheep's wool in their caps and girls seeking a post in domestic service would often carry a mop, hence the alternative name of these fairs.

Apart from seeking work, however, the hiring fairs also provided fun and relaxation for the workers during the week they were not employed. There were competitions of all kinds such as tossing the sheaf, wrestling, foot races, high jumps, trials of strength and skill, or, for the girls and women, a show of their skills in matters like making fine lace, creating samplers or baking bread, pies, cakes and making butter. There were displays of farm animals, and examples of the work of craftsmen in wood, metal and stone plus entertainment such as music, singing and dancing. Every type of rural activity could be represented at a hiring fair and so they became the main focus of what we might term holidays for the working people.

When they ceased to be a focus for those seeking work, they developed into occasions for amusement and enjoyment away from the workplace. Tests of practical and domestic skills predominated, but the fairs became more inclined towards local shows of produce, crafts and skills with enjoyable extras such as teas, music, dancing and local sports. Even when their original purpose had been forgotten, many retained the title of either hiring fair or mop fair. And that was the situation at Crampton.

Crampton Mop Fair with its accompanying ball was therefore a major event in the social calendar and as such, it was in my official diary as a venue to visit while on duty. The fair was always held on the afternoon of the first Saturday on or after 11 November—that was Martinmas, otherwise known as the feast day of St Martin of Tours—with some events being on the green and others inside the warmth of the hall. The ball followed in the evening with the buffet supper, and it usually started at 8 p.m. and finished at 11.45 p.m., with a local publican providing alcoholic drinks until 10.30 p.m., the end of licensing hours. At that time, dances and similar entertainment had to end before midnight due to the provisions of the Sunday Observance Acts. However, neither was the sort of event that would attract troublesome youths or travelling thieves, so I did not anticipate riots, drunkenness and vandalism. Even car-parking did not present a problem—there was ample free space around the village hall. It could therefore be argued that the presence of the local constable was not necessary, but if he failed to turn up in uniform at the mop fair, along with his wife and family, the organizers would want to know why he had neglected them. Apparently, it had been the practice since the days of the parish constable that he attend every Mop Fair. I was, therefore, part of ongoing history. The lord and lady of the manor, the local Catholic priest, the Anglican vicar, the member of parliament in whose constituency Crampton lay, the local doctor and his wife and their respective families were all expected to attend.

However, the constable was permitted to attend the ball in his civilian clothes, and be off duty, his official role in maintaining order having been completed. Even if Mary thought the whole affair was something of a chore, I considered it elevated the status of the local constable, but she was often asked to judge the infant school children's drawings that regularly included a policeman on traffic duty with his arms waving like a windmill. Such tasks of judging were fraught with danger—every mum would expect her offspring to win first prize or a special award, and eyebrows were raised if the same child won a prize year after year, or won more than one prize. Somehow, Mary coped with the delicate politics of such situations, but happily that first year, she was not a judge at the Mop Fair. That responsibility would surely follow once she was firmly settled into village routine.

However, as the village constable of Aidensfield, but also responsible for Crampton, I sallied forth to my first Mop Fair. I used my private car accompanied by Mary and our four children, one of whom was a tiny baby, and upon arrival discovered a parking space had been reserved for me. I thought that was a good start. Fortunately, I had taken the trouble to research my duties so knew what lay ahead. I was pleased to learn that I had no special responsibilities such as judging the cleanest pedal cycle or the best drawing of a prize sow.

Above the main door of the hall were two mops in the form of a large cross, and ahead for me lay the serious duty

31

of preventing children stealing angel cakes from displays, or watching out for competitors who might vandalize exhibits likely to beat those of their own family. Such possibilities warned me that the people treated the whole affair very seriously—winning a prize was almost a religion. Patrolling the display of exhibits with my hands behind my back and a fierce expression upon my face seemed to be one well-tried method of maintaining the Queen's Peace. Another was to take down the name of any troublemaker with a threat of future action. Few people and indeed fewer children liked their names and addresses being written in a policeman's notebook, and any threat of future action was very like the system of being bound over to keep the peace. If a miscreant behaved, nothing more would be heard about the affair; if they misbehaved, records of past misdemeanours would be resurrected along with some kind of suitable penalty.

Nonetheless, I knew I must always remember that determined young lads would sneak under the flaps of tents to grab an apple or pear from a display, or crawl beneath the tables in attempts to defy any restrictions relating to jelly, trifles, lemonade and ice cream.

The Mop Fair secretary was the highly popular and very efficient Mrs Pauline Chandler who was the vicar's wife. She did a splendid job, catering not only for the whims of the people, but also for the expectations of Lord and Lady Crampton and the other VIPs. She was very skilled at maintaining that delicate balance between pomposity and ordinariness. She would come and see whether I was having problems, pleading with me to help myself to cups of tea and cakes, and also ensuring my family was not abandoned when I was otherwise engaged. Mrs Chandler was ideal in her role and it was her verve and enthusiasm that made the Mop Fair such a success. She toured the displays and stalls, chatting to exhibitors and visitors alike, complimenting people on their cakes, drawings, paintings, papier-mâché sculptures, vegetables and fruit or whatever they had put on display. Her enthusiasm contributed to the success of the occasion and a bunch of flowers was her usual reward after the thank-you speeches. On my first visit, both the village green and the hall were packed with local people, amongst whom I noticed a young, dark-haired man wandering around on his own, taking photographs and writing comments in a notebook. He would be about twenty-five years old, I estimated.

His movements around the fair suggested he was a journalist, but I had never encountered him previously. He seemed very keen to talk to all the exhibitors and to take their photographs. He showed a close interest in almost everything and everyone, taking lots of personal pictures, particularly of attractive young women, as well as photographing many exhibits while promising to send photographs along when he had the time to develop them. I noticed he took no money in advance—people were told they could pay upon receipt and, in my view, that was an indication of his honesty. He took regular breaks for a cup of tea or a walk outside for fresh air and, as he did not show any interest in me, I did not like to interrupt him in his work.

I looked forward to reading his account in the *Gazette and Herald* or one of the other local newspapers. Not recognizing him as a local journalist, I reasoned that he could be a freelance, perhaps gathering information for an article. I felt that Mop Fair celebrations throughout Britain might make a good subject for an article or book.

'You should get your wife to visit Gypsy Lady Rose Leigh,' Mrs Chandler suggested during a lull, as I was enjoying a cup of tea and a slice of currant cake.

'Really, why?' I asked.

'She is both fascinating and very good, Mr Rhea. This is her first visit to Crampton. She was recommended to us by Eltering's October Feast Committee. Apparently she was a great success there.'

She indicated what looked like a miniature white and blue Arabian tent erected in a corner of the hall with multi-coloured flags fluttering around it. There was a small queue of women and girls outside; I had earlier wondered if it was the Ladies' Room. Evidently, it wasn't!

'What does she do?' I ventured.

'She reads palms and gives advice on personal matters,' she told me. 'Some ladies from Eltering were highly impressed by her predictions and character readings.'

'Does she live locally?' I asked.

'Really, I have no idea. She contacted me by telephone and asked if she could attend this fair and I told her she would be welcome, and that there was a small charge for placing a stall here. She said that was quite acceptable and she would pay on the day, which she has already done. She told me she had been to a show in Eltering with her demonstration—someone there had suggested Crampton's Mop Fair—and had also given a presentation to members of a luncheon club in Scarborough. With that kind of background, I felt she would be an asset and you can see by the queues that she is popular. Some of the Eltering ladies have come here for a second opportunity to meet her and I understand Gypsy Lady Leigh is to be the guest at a future Ladies' Luncheon Club in Ashfordly.'

'Fortune-telling, you mean? Is that what she does?'

'Well, yes, I suppose that was the old name for people like her, but she prefers to describe herself as a character assessor and personal adviser.'

'She doesn't read the future in tea-leaves then?' I smiled. 'Or resort to astrology?'

'Nothing like that, Mr Rhea. No, she's a true professional who can read palms and give advice accordingly. She is very discreet, as one expects from someone of her standing. She has stressed that every consultation is personal and very private.'

'I must admit I have never seen her in action anywhere else, or even heard about her. Perhaps she is a recent arrival in the area?'

'She did tell me she had recently moved to this part of Yorkshire, having come here from working in Bournemouth and along the south coast, although I think she has spent some time in Sheffield. You'll see by her noticeboard that she has led an interesting life.'

'Thanks. Well, I'll see if Mary is interested in her powers.' I thought I had better show some interest in this new attraction. 'She might forecast the numbers I need to win a fortune on the football pools.'

Prompted by Mrs Chandler's enthusiasm, I wandered through the displays to Gypsy Lady Rose Leigh's colourful tent and read the sign on a display board outside. It said: *Gypsy Lady Rose Leigh, the internationally renowned character assessor and palmist. Gypsy Lady Rose Leigh has just returned from a highly successful tour of Asia where she has been studying eastern techniques of identifying ancient influences that help to shape our lives. She is now delighted to be able to share her skills and discoveries with visitors and friends in England. Please come in for spell-binding and revealing advice at a very modest cost that may prove to be your personal investment for the future.* Underneath in very small print it said, *Rosa Galati was born of gypsy stock in Romania but, as a child in 1942, fled with her parents to the west when the Communists took control of her country. Safely settled in England she married the Laird Duncan Leigh of Strathfenton, since deceased.*

It sounded very impressive but sceptical police officers are always wary of people who make expansive claims about being able to forecast the future, read palms and perform other supposed miracles, especially for money! I was aware of the provisions of the Fraudulent Mediums Act of 1951 that extended to spiritualist mediums or persons using telepathy, clairvoyance and other powers for fraudulent purposes—but of course, that Act did not penalize those who performed for pure entertainment.

Likewise, the Vagrancy Act of 1824, still in force during my tenure at Aidensfield, contained an offence that was committed when anyone pretended or professed to tell fortunes, or used any subtle craft, means or device by palmistry or otherwise to deceive or impose on any of Her Majesty's subjects. Such persons were punished as rogues and vagabonds.

So, if this lady was performing purely for entertainment, then she was quite within the law, but if she was intending to deceive people, especially for a reward of some kind, then she might be culpable. Or was I being over-cautious, too zealous or even a spoil-sport? After all, this fair was an occasion for fun and happiness and I had no wish to ruin that atmosphere. Nonetheless, I had a job to do.

My brief was to protect the public so I decided Mary could put the gypsy lady to the test. I knew that if I went into her tent for a reading she would not behave in her normal manner, an impossible act with a uniformed policeman sitting there. I took Mary aside; the children were being temporarily cared for by our babysitter, Mrs Quarry, who had arrived at the fair, apparently determined that all our children should have another ice cream. She would also be looking after them tonight while we went to the ball.

'Can you go and get a reading or consultation, or whatever it's called, from Gypsy Lady Rose?' I asked Mary.

'What on earth for, Nick? I know you think such things are a load of rubbish so why do you want me to do that?'

'I just want to know if she's breaking the law, taking people for a ride, getting money by pretending to tell fortunes, or something similar. A confidence trickster in other words.'

'Nick, this is a village fair: people come here for a bit of fun, they don't mind someone like Gypsy Lady Rose telling them they are soon to meet a tall, dark, handsome stranger, or that lady luck might be shining on them. And they don't object to crossing her palm with silver in order to enjoy the experience. It's just the same at the seaside, there are dozens of fortune tellers called Gypsy Rose Lee, all quite harmless.'

'Exactly!' I said. 'I am aware of all that, but I just want to be sure that innocent people here today are not being conned.'

'You're supposed to be here enjoying yourself, not worrying about performing your duty!'

'I am on duty,' I reminded her. 'I'm here to prevent crime, protect the public and preserve the Queen's Peace. That's why I was invited and why I am wearing my uniform. So I want to know what that woman is up to. It might all be innocent stuff—'

'All right, I'll do it, but just for you! But I'll need money to give her—you can call it expenses!' and Mary held out her hand.

I crossed her palm with silver—a half-crown to be precise—and off she went. She joined the queue of other hopefuls, all women and girls standing at a barrier some distance from the tent—I guessed that was to prevent anyone overhearing the confidential conversations, something akin to a confessional.

Happy that I done something positive in the course of my duty, I continued my patrol. I decided to go outside for some fresh air, but likewise I wanted to undertake a discreet check of my own. I knew from my years in the police service at Strensford that Gypsy Rose Lee (not Leigh) was a regular attraction during the height of the summer season. She had a small kiosk at the inshore end of the West Pier and performed in much the same way as the woman now in Crampton Mop Fair. And, of course, there were many Gypsy Rose Lees around the country—indeed there had been lots of them in Strensford, Scarborough, Whitby and Bridlington over the years.

Every season seemed to attract a different woman claiming to be the original Gypsy Rose Lee. So who was the woman now sitting in our Mop Fair? Was she one of the many Gypsy Rose Lees? Her surname was differently spelled, so was Leigh her real name? I thought it quite possible she was one of the seaside fortune tellers particularly as our Mop Fair was held in November, far from the bustle of the summer season. Perhaps attendance at such fairs was a means of maintaining an income during the winter? But if she was not breaking any laws, then I had no right to be critical of her and her activities. Nonetheless I was very curious and, if I was honest, I needed something to occupy me during my time at the fair. There was a lot of hanging around and chatting while looking important, so delving into the background of our Gypsy Lady Rose Leigh might provide an interesting diversion.

I thought I would start with her car. She must have used a car or van to transport herself, her equipment, costume and the tent she was using. If so, it would be on the car park reserved for stallholders. There were parking spaces for guests, stallholders, exhibitors and the general public, all free. As I wandered around, I noticed the photographer heading my way. He smiled at me but made no further comment, then went to a green Ford van, unlocked it and reached inside. It was the sort of vehicle used by greengrocers or butchers, but its two windows in the outward opening rear doors were both blacked out. It was impossible to see the contents of the rear section. That was not particularly unusual—lots of vehicles had windows of that kind and perhaps he processed his films in there.

'Films,' he smiled as if to explain his presence. 'I need more films. I've run out already but I've plenty of spares in here.'

'Are you the local press?' This was an opportunity to find out more about him.

'No,' he said. 'I'm collecting material for a book about mop fairs and similar rural events across the country. I also write freelance pieces for rural magazines. This visit is part of my ongoing research.'

'What a good idea, keeping accounts of those events alive and in our memories,' I smiled. 'Was this one any different from the others?'

'Not really; they're all pretty much the same, although there are slight variations locally. Here, for example, I loved the stall with the home-made Crampton cheese, and it was amazing how many children had painted pigs, hens and sheep. In towns they paint buses, shops and traffic lights.'

He did not volunteer his name, but if I really wanted it, I could obtain that from the registration number of his van. He unlocked the driver's door, took a handful of spools from a haversack that was lying on the front seat, and locked up.

We chatted only for a minute or two before he said he must return to the fray, and, light-heartedly, I said I would guard the cars against thieves and vandals. But when he'd left me, I jotted down the registration number of his van—123 PXO. It was the only van among all the cars in the car park.

I did not find any vehicle that I could presume belonged to Gypsy Lady Rose Leigh—perhaps she got changed in the ladies' cloakroom when she arrived? She could carry her clothing in the boot of any car, however small, but how did she transport that tent and all her associated paraphernalia? Perhaps someone had brought her and would collect her afterwards? Certainly there was no gypsy caravan with a horse.

Somewhat baffled, I returned to the hall where I saw the photographer was taking more pictures and chatting to recent arrivals. As the afternoon wore on, and as the late autumn darkness descended, people began to drift away from the fair. Most would be heading home to prepare for tonight's ball, and that was the signal for the stallholders to start dismantling their displays. But Gypsy Lady Rose Leigh was still busy. Mary had now reached the front of the queue and I was in time to see her enter the colourful tent. She would be in there for some ten minutes, I guessed, and there was only one other woman waiting. Behind that final hopeful client was a 'closed' notice on a stand: Mary had got there just in time.

I completed what I hoped was the final tour of the fair, noting the emptying stalls with some proudly bearing small placards proclaiming they had won a prize. Mrs Chandler came up to me to express gratitude for my presence, and I told her Mary was still with Gypsy Lady Rose while Mrs Quarry was entertaining our children to their last ice cream of the day.

The photographer was also preparing to leave and he waved at me, saying, 'Thanks, I enjoyed that. I've got to go home to get ready for the ball—more souvenir photographs there no doubt!'

And he left.

As the crowds rapidly dwindled, I waited for Mary as Mrs Quarry said, 'I'll get the children into the car, Nick.

Mary won't be long, and my husband will be coming to collect me. See you all tonight? I'll be at your house for half past seven.'

'Thanks, it's good of you; without you, we'd never get a night out!'

She left me as she led our little ones outside to my car and within a few minutes, Mary emerged from the fortune-teller's tent.

'So how was that?' I asked, as I led her to a quiet corner of the hall.

'Nothing special.' She shrugged her shoulders. 'I suppose it was what I expected—she read my palm and said my life-line showed I could look forward to old age and she told me all sorts of rubbish based on readings of my head line and fate line; then she came out with the old and well-tested routine of saying I would soon meet a dark stranger who would offer me a wonderful, fulfilled and happy future, and she advised me to take care of my health and to make use of violet colours in my clothing. She said violet would enhance my skin and eyes. I had taken my wedding ring off, by the way, so she did not know I was married with four children—and she never mentioned that.'

'So you were not impressed?'

'Not at all. It was just the sort of rubbish I'd heard when I was a teenager visiting Scarborough. And it cost me two shillings.'

'Did she try to get you to part with money for anything else? Or promises of great wealth if you invested money with her, or a one pound note to take part in some foreign sweepstake because she'd read it in your stars that this was your lucky time?'

'No, Nick, nothing like that. I thought she was typical of people who earn their living in that way.'

'What did she look like? Was she realistic? I mean, do you think she really was a gypsy or a refugee from Romania?'

'It's very hard to say. It was dark inside her tent, just a low light and a couple of small candles. She used a small table covered with a gaudy cloth and there was a glass crystal ball, for effect no doubt. She was dressed in what looked like Arabian robes with a headdress that covered her hair and mouth. Only her eyes were visible, but she did have white skin. I could see the skin around her eyes and on her hands. Her nails were painted red, by the way and she wore no rings. And she spoke like a Yorkshire woman from Leeds, or somewhere in the West Riding, not like someone from the North Riding. I didn't think her accent was at all foreign.'

'How old was she? Could you tell?'

'Not really. Her hands looked like those of a young woman—by that I mean someone less than thirty, and so did the skin around her eyes. She wasn't an old woman, Nick, that's for sure.'

'So the whole experience was quite atmospheric?'

'Not really, to be honest. For impressionable youngsters it might have been, but for me it was all a bit tawdry. My impression is that she was just being an entertainer of the old school, nothing more than that. She said nothing offensive and did not exert any pressure on me at all. It was just a cosy meeting in a strange situation, especially for Crampton!'

'Ah, well, I had to carry out the check, so thanks. So do we know her real name? Did she give you a business card with her name, address and phone number?'

'No, nothing. As I left she wished me good luck and said violet was my lucky colour, that was all.'

'Fair enough, I'm happy now. I've done my duty. So, shall we go home and get the children their teas, then get ready for the ball?'

Although there was to be a buffet supper at the ball, Mary made a light tea that was primarily for the children who would miss the buffet. A couple of hours later, with Mary in her best dress and me in a new dark suit, she and I returned to Crampton in the darkness of that November night. Both of us loved ballroom dancing and it was nice to have an evening out; we looked forward to the event. In the glow from the single lamp shining over the car park, I left my car in the space I had used earlier and noticed the photographer's green van was also occupying the space it had earlier used.

He must have managed to get home, get changed and get back here in time for the start of the ball, although I had no idea where he lived. Then I wondered if Gypsy Lady Rose Leigh would be attending? If so, would anyone recognize her when not wearing her 'working' clothes? But I could not see any car or van that might belong to her. Shortly after we entered the body of the hall, now cleared of all its stalls and displays, the tempo began to warm up as more people arrived. They took to the floor as a very musical five-piece band played for the range of dances. Then, as Mary went to chat to a friend, I noticed Mrs Chandler nursing a glass of dry Martini. We exchanged pleasantries and then I commented, 'I enjoyed the fair today, Mrs Chandler, it's so nice seeing the whole village involved and enjoying themselves.'

'With nothing for you to worry about either!' She smiled. 'We are a law-abiding lot, you know. But we've always thought the presence of our local bobby was wise; that has always been an essential part of our strategy. We regard you as a vital part of the event. Your presence was the continuation of a very ancient custom.'

'The uniform alone can work wonders,' I smiled. 'My wife was quite taken with Gypsy Lady Rose Leigh.'

I decided to find out more about this mysterious woman. Mrs Chandler would surely know a little of her background. I felt there was something about Gypsy Lady Rose that was not quite right, but could not quite determine what it was—but something was gnawing at me. I felt the fortune-teller needed a little extra investigation and had decided that while getting ready for the ball. It was the wording on the board outside her tent that had bothered me. It had contained one or two errors that might have been nothing more than carelessness by the sign-writer or by the originator of the wording, or it could have been something calculated to deceive. And I thought it odd that no one knew who she was or where she had come from.

'Will she be here?' I asked Mrs Chandler.

'No, she couldn't come, she went home with her husband.'

'Husband?'

'The man taking the photographs. He goes almost everywhere with her, drives her to her venues and takes photographs to record the occasion while researching the books he writes. He took her home and now he's come back for the ball as he wants to take more photos. People like buying his pictures as a memento of happy times.'

'I never did find out his name, so where do they live?'

'Somewhere near Scarborough, she told me. One of the villages near the town. Scalby, I think. And I don't know their names either.'

I could trace their address through the registration number of the van, but not tonight. The Local Taxation Office at Northallerton maintained the county records of motor vehicles registered within its area, but the office would be shut over the weekend. In an emergency, I could ask a constable from Northallerton town's police station to go around and check the records—they kept keys for urgent research out of hours—but I did not consider this to be an emergency. I would send off the usual request card, known as an HO/RT/1 on Monday. As I talked to Mrs Chandler with the band playing in the background, Mary reappeared at my side after chatting to her friend.

'Nick,' she chided me, 'forget work. We're here to enjoy ourselves, not for you to pretend you're a great detective. Leave that poor gypsy woman alone! You're obsessed with her, but she's not harming anyone. Come along, I want to do this foxtrot.'

I did my best to appear as if I was not thinking about my work as I danced several dances with Mary and some with our female friends. The band was good and maintained the correct tempo for dances both old and modern, but I could not eradicate my suspicions about the gypsy woman. I began to wonder if I was really being obsessive, but during a short interval, I decided to have a walk around the car park—exactly the sort of thing I would normally have done had I been on duty, just for the purpose of carrying out a brief visual security check of the vehicles. It was approaching eleven o'clock with the band taking their last five-minute break and Mary had gone for a chat to a friend she had noticed across the room. She wouldn't miss me.

The car park was behind the hall and was lit by a solitary light fixed to the rear of the building, and tonight every space was occupied. As I walked among the vehicles, I saw nothing that would raise my concern—no vandalized cars, no cars with out-of-date excise licence discs, no cars with dangerous parts and none with sleeping dogs or children inside. In other words, things were absolutely as they should be. As I walked past the photographer's van, however, I thought I sensed a movement or slight noise inside the rear portion with its shaded windows. It was the sort of impression I might have had if there was a dog inside, perhaps switching positions while asleep, or even moving to see what was happening outside. Noting that the photographer was not near the van or in the driving compartment, I decided to sneak a quick look, but the darkness surrounding the vehicle and its shaded interior meant it was impossible—and I did not have my police torch with me. Nonetheless, I could see the rear compartment was full of something—his equipment I guessed—and I caught sight of some colourful cushions on the floor and brightly designed scarves hanging from coat-hangers in the rear. The hangers were fixed to the struts of the side panels in the rear albeit close to the front of the van. It appeared as if the van served two purposes—one as a darkroom for the photographer, and the other as a changing room or place of rest for Gypsy Lady Rose Leigh.

So had the gypsy lady gone home as Mrs Chandler had thought, or was she sleeping here until her husband had completed his work? I was sure there was something or someone in the rear of that van, but it was not within the scope of my duty to make a fuss.

After all as Mary had said, what harm was she doing? Besides, the occupant might be the family dog even if it did not bark at my presence. Refreshed by my amble around the exterior I returned to the fray where Mary was waiting.

'Where have you been?' she demanded.

'Outside for some fresh air.'

'You've been a long time. The band's back and I could do with a nice modern waltz . . .'

And so the mood of the evening was maintained. We returned home feeling tired but happy. It was just as I was going up to bed that the telephone rang. It was about quarter past twelve and the caller was Charles Denton from Crampton.

'I hope I've caught you in time, Mr Rhea, before you got to bed. I saw you at the Mop Ball but I'm afraid it's bad news. We were burgled while we were out.'

'Has anything been taken?'

'Yes, some of my wife's jewellery and a pair of antique silver candlesticks, they knew what to take.'

'I'll come straight away,' I assured him.

The house was quite isolated on the edge of Crampton and entry had been made through a rear ground-floor sash window. The intruder had smashed the glass to release the window catch, raised the bottom half and climbed through. There were indistinct footprints on the window ledge and some deposits of soil from the garden beneath and the window was still open. Mr and Mrs Denton showed me the trail of footprints from the utility room where the burglar had entered, through the kitchen, into the dining room where he had taken the candlesticks, and then upstairs to the master bedroom where he had found Sylvia Denton's jewellery box. Not everything had been taken, merely a selection of the best, and the box had been left behind. The Dentons told me they had not left any lights on in the house while they were out, so the burglar must have used a torch. I made a list of the stolen goods with a detailed description of each item.

'I'd like our Scenes of Crime Officers to come and check for fingerprints and other evidence, but that won't be till morning. They'll want to check your jewellery box, Mrs

Denton, the dining room and other places, especially the point of entry. Can you leave things alone for tonight? Don't disturb anything and don't dust the surfaces in the morning!'

'Yes, I understand; we can use the spare room tonight.'

I commiserated with them and said I would circulate a description of the stolen items when I returned home. But even before I left the Denton's house, their phone rang. It was Mary—she said there had been another burglary at the home of Mr and Mrs Simpson in Crampton. They had just got home and had called the police house so I asked Mary to assure them I would be there in five or ten minutes.

I knew the Simpsons' house: it was called Fir Trees and was in the centre of the village. There it was a very similar story. They had attended the ball and had gone back to some friends for a nightcap before returning home in the early hours of Sunday to find the kitchen window catch had been forced, and jewellery and some antique silver cutlery stolen. They'd not left any lights on during their absence. As before, I listed and described all the stolen property and told the couple that our Scenes of Crime Officers would attend tomorrow morning.

Back at home, I rang the night duty officer in the Scenes of Crime Department and booked a team to visit Crampton as soon as practicable, then circulated a description of the missing items to all mobiles and beat officers on duty throughout the county. They would stop and search any sus-pect vehicles and people encountered during the night, but it seemed that these crimes had been committed by a local person who knew the houses would be unoccupied during the period of the Mop Fair Ball.

Then a third person—Jack Welford—rang me at seven o'clock on Sunday morning to report yet another burglary while he and his wife Susan had been at the ball on Saturday evening. For me, I'd had only an hour or two in bed, but when I questioned him, I found it was a repetition of the previous two cases. I began to worry that we might have an enterprising burglar living in Crampton or one of the neigh-bouring villages.

After acquainting Sergeant Blaketon by phone with this sudden rural crime wave, I completed all the necessary procedures as the Scenes of Crime Officers arrived in the village to undertake their duties. Three scenes of crime in a small place like Crampton! It seemed unbelievable. I rang our local Criminal Record Office in an attempt to discover whether we had any known or suspected burglars who had recently come to live in Crampton or nearby, but their answer was negative.

As I waited outside the respective houses in Crampton while the SOCO team did their specialized work, I thought about the events of the last few hours. The evidence to date suggested an opportunist travelling burglar, but it did not rule out the possibility that one was living in or near Crampton without my knowledge. A recent arrival perhaps? Had such a villain realized that most of the resident population would be attending the ball and had he managed to locate a small but valuable selection of target premises, very easy when houses did not have any interior lights showing in the evening, other than a porch light? Raiding them would not be difficult due to their isolated location and the fact it was dark. Few, if any, would have burglar-proof windows or doors. Even so, the presence of a stranger in the village last night might have been noticed—Crampton was very compact and all the residents knew one another.

And then I realized strangers *had* visited Crampton last night: it was the photographer and his wife, the mysterious Gypsy Lady Rose Leigh. I had been slightly suspicious of the fortune-teller because of irregularities on her noticeboard. I recalled from my school history lessons that the Communists had invaded Romania in 1946, not 1942 as shown on her advertisement (I remembered because we had a refugee from Romania in our class at school). And I knew of no place in Scotland bearing the name of Strathfenton. I had also wondered how a refugee living in England had managed to marry a Scottish laird . . . if her board had said, 'Britain' instead of England, then that could have made sense. I knew, of course, that a woman living in England could have met and married someone from Scotland but those small uncertainties had combined to alert me.

Then there was the photographer's van. I was sure someone had been hiding inside it when I had inspected it last night . . . and, I then realized, the photographer had taken people's names and addresses during the fair on the promise of sending them photographs. And he had also attended the ball to undertake a similar exercise—was that his alibi? In addition, it was almost by chance that I had discovered the link between him and the fortune-teller. While the SOCO team was working inside the Welfords' house, I took the opportunity to speak to Jack, a dour sixty-year-old woodman who worked on Crampton Estate.

'Were you both at the Mop Fair yesterday?'

'Aye, Mr Rhea, we were. And the ball afterwards.'

'Did you have your photographs taken?'

'Aye we did, at the fair but not at the ball. We didn't want a second lot.'

'And did the photographer take your names and address?'

'He did, he said he'd send a selection of proofs to us when they were ready. There was nothing to pay yet, he said, we could settle up when we selected the ones we wanted and made a firm order.'

'Did he give his name and address?'

'Come to think of it, no he didn't. He took our details but never gave his own.'

'And did he ask if you were going to the ball later?'

'Aye, he did, so he said he would try not to bother us about getting another set of pictures. But he couldn't have done our burglary, Mr Rhea, he was at the ball the whole time we were there.'

'He was indeed,' I agreed, now deciding to ask the same questions from the Simpsons and the Dentons. And they gave identical answers.

Now it was becoming very possible that the photographer could not have committed the crimes because he was at the ball the whole time, but it was equally clear that he could have been the burglar's accomplice. During his time at the fair he could have obtained the names and addresses of houses that would be unoccupied during the ball—say 8 p.m. until about midnight—and then his accomplice would have visited them under cover of the November night, entering those that were in complete darkness.

Those with interior lights showing might have had babysitters or other people on the premises and would not be attacked. But the best thing I had done was to note the registration number of the photographer's van, although not yet having had the opportunity to send off the HO/RT/1, or to telephone the Local Taxation Office to check the registered owner's name and address. Today, being a Sunday, it would be closed, but I would have to act swiftly.

If the photographer and his fortune-telling wife were a burglary team, we must try and catch them with the stolen goods still in their possession. That was the finest possible proof. And we would have to examine records of burglaries or other crimes at more venues where they had jointly performed. I recalled from Mrs Chandler's conversation with me last night that the couple lived near Scarborough, possibly in Scalby on the outskirts, and so I decided to ring Scarborough CID. Officers would be working today and so, rather than use the telephones of the victims, I went to the village kiosk and reversed the charges. That was easier and swifter than driving home to make the call—a radio call would not be so efficient because it would go into Scarborough's Control Room and I would not be able to talk directly with CID.

After a conversation with the operator in York Telephone Exchange, she said she would connect me with the switchboard at Scarborough's police station in Northway who would have to consent to the reversed charge before my call could be accepted. When I explained the situation, the Scarborough switchboard operator accepted my call and put me through to CID.

'Scarborough CID,' answered a woman's voice.

'Is Detective Sergeant Newton there?' I asked. 'It's PC Rhea from Aidensfield, and it is urgent.'

'Yes, hang on a minute,' and I heard her shout across the room, 'Sarge, it's PC Rhea from Aidensfield; he says it's urgent.'

There was a short lull then a deep voice said, 'Now, Nick. What have you got for us?'

I told him the full story, emphasizing the links with Scarborough and Scalby, and at the end emphasized the registration number 123 PXO.

'Because the LTO is closed over the weekend, I haven't had the opportunity to check the number,' I explained. 'But if the stolen goods were transported from Crampton after the ball, they might still be in that van. And if it was used to convey our stolen goods, it could have been involved in other similar burglaries where the couple were operating as a team.'

'Great, Nick. Leave it with me. It's a quiet Sunday morning here for a change. I'll get on to it immediately. I can get access to the LTO through CID at Northallerton. If we do find stolen goods, we'll need your victims to come and identify what might be their belongings. I'll call you back as soon as possible.'

Having spoken to Alec Newton, I went to tell the Simpsons, the Welfords and the Dentons and explain what I had done and why I had taken those steps. In all cases, SOCO had finished its own investigation and had found some useful fingerprints and other evidence in the attacked premises. I would now head for Ashfordly Police Station to record the crimes in our register and circulate a detailed description of the stolen property.

When I arrived there was no duty constable in the office but Sergeant Blaketon was at the counter. 'It's Ventress's day off,' he explained. 'And Foxton is investigating the source of a small fire in The Ashfordly Hotel. Sorry I couldn't leave the office to get over to Crampton to assist you at those scenes of crime, but I knew I could rely on you.'

'A fire, Sarge?'

'Yes but we don't think it was arson, more of an electrical fault in the kitchens. So, how's the burglary investigation progressing? Do we need to call in CID?'

'I don't think so.' I then provided a full account of my morning's efforts and he smiled.

'Good, so we await the outcome of Scarborough's finest?'

Because my duties last night and my efforts so far today had amounted almost to a full tour of duty, Sergeant Blaketon told me to go home to complete my files. It was while there, that Alec Newton rang from Scarborough CID.

'Great news, Nick. We found the stuff in a loft at Scalby. At first they denied everything but we found a single silver spoon in the back of their van—it had got down a groove between the floor and a side panel—so we decided to search the entire house. It was a goldmine, Nick: they've clearly been at it for a long time—jewellery, silverware and antiques seem to be their speciality. They dispose of it through unsuspecting antique shops and second-hand dealers.'

'So who are they?'

'A couple of professional villains from Sheffield called Baines—John and Jessica—confidence tricksters and skilled burglars who thought it was getting too hot for them in Sheffield and who came to Scalby a year or so ago. The wife does the burgling, she's small enough to get through most windows. The husband sets up the crime, establishes an alibi and so on, obtains the addresses of empty premises by his photography scam.'

'They've clearly been caught before?'

'Yes, but not through executing this scam. They had other tricks. So, well done. You can tell your customers in Crampton that we'll be in touch soon to ask them to come and identify their own property.'

'A fair cop, in other words?' I joked.

3. MY FAIR LADY

Many of the old-fashioned fairs were established by ancient charter, peaceful gatherings that concentrated upon modest commercial enterprises of a very local nature, usually with some accompanying entertainment. Home-grown or locally made produce was on sale and included commodities such as eggs, confectionery, vegetables, fruit, bread, pies and livestock. Shoes and clothes were also sold at these fairs with the distinction between fairs and markets sometimes being rather blurred. I think we can say that a market with added amusements, competitions or entertainment could be described as a fair. Many of the early fairs were established before the Reformation to celebrate the feast day of a local saint or patron saint of the Catholic Church. Indeed, the word 'fair' is derived from *feria* meaning holy day. Some fairs specialized in cheese, fish or even geese, sheep or horses, although their ancient origins were often associated with the hiring of workers.

As we saw in the previous chapter, those were sometimes called mop fairs that were used by people seeking employment or wishing to acquire staff. The idea of having fun at the fair instead of it being a serious commercial event was in many cases incidental, but with the passage of time the idea of extra attractions such as entertainment, music and dancing became a vital part of all fairs. In time, funfairs became the norm, either travelling from place to place, or being established permanently in popular seaside resorts. They bear little or no resemblance to the fairs of ancient times. Certainly by the 1960s, many fairs comprised a range of market stalls along with family entertainment with no thought of them being a source of finding or providing work. The notion of 'hiring fairs' had ceased although mop fairs continued if only by name.

However, there was a different type of fair the impending arrival of which, often on an annual basis at a particular date, generally brought a sense of foreboding to the local community. If young people looked forward to enjoying the fun of such a fair, then adults did not usually share their enthusiasm. As the traditional fairs began to fade from the scene along with the decline in celebrating saints' days, they were replaced by noisy, brash and very large cavalcades of garish vehicles and equipment known as funfairs or travelling fairs.

Many claimed they were descended from traditional hiring fairs, in the sense that they provided fun, games and amusement for ordinary people, but goods like food, clothes and crafts formed no part of their business. The noise, dirt, litter and problems they invariably attracted made them unwelcome among a large section of the community. They seemed to appeal to the less desirable sections of our society even though most of the travellers were essentially decent and law-abiding, even if they followed a somewhat unusual way of life, living in caravans and always on the move.

When a modern travelling fair was due in town, members of the public would complain vociferously through the correspondence columns of their local newspapers, but there was very little anyone could do to prevent its arrival. It travelled towns where the right to hold a fair had been established by ancient charter—but the word 'fair' in this case was very loosely defined. Fun fairs bear very little resemblance to the fairs of former times and it might be argued that those ancient charters do not include them.

Once a fair has been established by ancient charter it can be cancelled only by order of the Home Secretary or by Act of Parliament and that kind of action could be political suicide both at parliamentary and local council level. All kinds of hidden discriminatory messages and political implications could be read into the abolition of a fair. So, the fairs continued even if they had degenerated into the type of funfair one associates with the seaside along with its dodgems, big dippers, amusement arcades, coconut shies, merry-go-rounds, rifle ranges, candy floss and constant loud music with the distinctive sound of a fairground organ.

It was this kind of fair that arrived in Brantsford every year on or about the feast of Saints Gervase and Protase. These two saints were always associated with one another because they had been martyred together in Milan in AD 386 and their feast day was celebrated on 19 June. Although they were saints in the Roman Catholic calendar with no links to England, for some unfathomable reason they were patrons of Brantsford's ancient parish church. Over the years, the simple fair that had in times past helped to celebrate their feast day had been replaced by a giant travelling-circus type of entertainment that had no association with either churches or saints. While on the road it comprised dozens of vehicles large and small, including pantechnicons, living vans and a squad of cars. Once it reached its destination, the convoy spewed out dismantled stalls and items of machinery that were quickly turned into shooting galleries, coconut shies, darts challenges, coin-operated amusement arcades, dodgems, merry-go-rounds and a host of other facilities. This type of funfair occupied a huge amount of space, often in the market-place or some other convenient site and, of course, it was accompanied by loud, jolly music.

The Gervase and Protase Fair always opened on the Monday nearest the saints' feast day and remained until the following Saturday. It shut down in the early hours of

Sunday morning and moved overnight to another location ready for its components to be assembled to begin all over again on the Monday morning. I am sure its operators had no thoughts of celebrating saints' days. While in Brantsford it occupied the entire market-place and so for the whole of that week the day-to-day routine of the quiet little town was disrupted. Market-day had to be cancelled, for example, because there was nowhere large enough to accommodate its regular stallholders; car-parking in the town centre became impossible and businesses suffered because customers from outlying villages drove elsewhere to do their shopping. Market towns like Eltering and Ashfordly basked in the benefits, if only for a short while.

Having aired their advance grumbles in the local paper, once the fair was up and running, local residents complained about the incessant noise from the music and machinery. That was not surprising because it continued until one or two o'clock every morning. Rowdy young people shouted and sang in the town centre too, having spent time in the pubs drinking to foment some false courage so they could confront the fairground people. It all meant that, in the town centre, sleep became impossible during the Gervase and Protase Fair and most people went elsewhere to avoid such tribulations. Indeed, a lot of townspeople took their summer holiday during that week.

Because Brantsford was within the police sub-division that included Eltering and Ashfordly, the town's policing during the fair involved every officer serving in that police area. Throughout the duration of the G & P Fair, as it had become known, there was a permanent police presence. Although this afforded some protection for the fairground personnel and their equipment, that was not our prime purpose. The police presence was intended to benefit everyone while deterring troublemakers, violence and vandalism. Some of the troublemakers lived in the town, but others came into Brantsford during the week of the fair, quite deliberately to cause bother.

Although the fairground personnel themselves did not cause undue policing problems, they did receive unwelcome attention from both incoming and resident youths. Not surprisingly, the fairground workers considered it natural and sensible to protect themselves, their women, their vehicles and their expensive equipment, and because of their constant movement around the country, they had become very experienced in dealing with trouble if and when it arose.

No one in authority could quite understand the compulsion of local youths to attack the fairground and its workers, but in the opinion of local police officers it was because the fair attracted crowds of very attractive teenage girls and unattached young women. With many youthful men and girls at the peak of their love and lust years, it was an unfortunate fact that the girls regarded the fairground workers as infinitely more attractive and romantic than the local youths. There was something about them that girls found highly interesting and most appealing.

Perhaps it was their dark, romantic appearance, their lifestyle on the open road, their defiance of convention and flouting of rules, or their ability to make people happy and provide constant enjoyment. There is no doubt many of them could be utterly charming when it suited them. Certainly there was a propensity to give impressionable young girls free rides on the fairground equipment and to show them how to win on the amusement machines.

At times, the fairground lads would join the girls on dangerous rides or the dodgems, putting protective arms around them to prevent accidents; they'd do likewise when showing the girls how to fire rifles on the ranges or throw darts. The girls loved that kind of close and intimate attention. In short, they loved the fair and everything it represented.

Little wonder, therefore, that the local lads resented the presence of the handsome, daring and romantic in-comers. The local tribe could re-establish their superiority in the only way that was available to them—by thrashing the invaders physically. No wonder the fairs had special guards during the time they were closed, especially during the hours of darkness. It was, therefore, necessary for police officers to patrol the fairground and its environs day and night throughout its week in Brantsford. although it was accepted that many fairground workers regarded the officers with animosity. They considered them agents of the British establishment, there to protect their own kind. Despite our role as impartial peacekeepers between two warring tribes, I never knew a fairground worker, male or female, who invited a policeman into a caravan for a cup of tea, or to shelter in bad weather. Furthermore, they seldom volunteered information if the police were carrying out an enquiry of any kind. Dealing with fairground workers was therefore like treading on eggshells and it was amazing how many were called Smith.

My first experience with the G & P Fair was destined to be on the Tuesday after its arrival. That morning I was in Ashfordly Police Station prior to driving out to Brantsford when I noticed a message that had come from Strensford Police. The fact it had arrived through the post suggested it was not urgent, but it had been circulated to all stations via the official Crime Information Sheets. It concerned a fifteen-year-old girl who was missing from home. There was no suggestion she had been kidnapped, or that she was in dire danger, because it was thought she had run away to join a travelling fair that had been visiting Filey on the East Riding stretch of the Yorkshire coast. She was a few weeks short of her sixteenth birthday and Strensford Police had circulated the message because she was still under the age of consent and regarded by the laws of the time as a 'young person'. That meant she was subject to a wide range of protective laws, particularly because she was female. If an adult ran away to join a circus or a fair, there would be little or no police action to trace him or her, unless the person was either a victim of crime or suspected of crime. But the situation was different so far as young people were concerned, girls in particular.

The missing girl's name was Kay Goodwin. According to the information received from Strensford Police she was from a good background, an only child, with a caring mother. She had never been in trouble with the police and attended a local secondary school where she was considered an ideal pupil, being intelligent, pleasant and hard-working.

The girl's home was clean and tidy with ample clothes and food, but when things went wrong with their children to the extent of involving the police, it was common for parents to make an assurance that until that moment, everything within the home was peaceful and calm with no problems. They would assure the police they had had no trouble with their children even if they were truly an almighty parental headache. They did not want the police to think it was the parents who could not cope. Thus, the reasons provided by parents as explanations for their teenage girls running away from home were always treated with caution.

For no apparent reason, therefore, Kay had disappeared after school on the previous Friday without leaving any kind of message. It was one of her close friends who had said she had run off to join a travelling fair at Filey. The friend could not elaborate—it had been something Kay had mentioned in an unguarded moment. In the circular, Strensford Police had provided a description of her along with a black-and-white photograph of her in a party dress. In the photo she looked like a child—in fact, she looked about twelve or thirteen—but no date or age was given for that photo. She was described as being 5 feet 4 inches tall, average build with fair hair and blue eyes. Her hair was long and worn in a pony-tail, but sometimes she would plait it over her head. She had clearly intended to run away because she had taken all the cash from her money-box in her bedroom—thought to be about £25—as well as some spare clothes, nightwear, toothbrush and make-up. It was thought she would be wearing a pale-green dress and a darker green cardigan, brown shoes and possibly a brown kagoul borrowed from a friend. An added item said that when she was made-up she could look older than her years, able to pass herself off as eighteen. That made me wonder about the accuracy and real value of the photograph we had received. Probably, she looked nothing like that, especially if she had run away and could make herself look older than her true age. The note concluded by adding that enquiries had been made in Filey by the East Riding of Yorkshire Constabulary, but by the time they had received information about Kay's disappearance, the fair had left for an unknown destination.

As I studied the message and dealt with the other items in the post, Sergeant Blaketon emerged from his office. I passed him the information about Kay Goodwin whereupon he said, 'You'll be checking that fair in Brantsford today? Wasn't it somewhere in the Scarborough area last week? I recall something about it in the papers. I reckon it might have been the one at Filey. There aren't many travelling fairs around here. Check it out to see whether the lass is there.'

'Right, Sergeant.'

'Good. Was there anything else in the post? Have you any reports outstanding?'

'Nothing is the answer to both questions, Sergeant.'

'Good, well I won't detain you. Do what you can to trace that girl, although I doubt if you'll get any useful information from the fairground people. They're not noted for being co-operative with the police, but it would be useful to ascertain that she is *not* there.'

'Do we know if there are any other fairs in our area?' I asked.

'Not that I am aware of. We do get them passing through from time to time and nicking turnips from the roadside fields, but the Brantsford fair is our only one at the moment.'

'It's odd how many girls run away to join a fair or a circus although I am aware that certain family matters are not talked about outside the happy home.'

'It happens, Rhea—the evil stepfather syndrome. Parents want to keep it in the family, not let the outside world know things are wrong. That's their usual response. But such things happen these days as they always have done. That message doesn't tell us whether the missing girl has a father or a stepfather, but that shouldn't affect our enquiries. All we want to know is whether she's at Brantsford, travelling with that fair.'

'We don't know much of the background to this case, do we?'

'We don't need to, Rhea, it's not our problem. We don't need a family history to carry out a simple check. I know and you know that stepfathers have been known to interfere sexually with their stepdaughters and even fathers with their natural daughters, but I am sure our Strensford colleagues will be looking into those possibilities. She wouldn't run away without good reason. But finding out why the girl left home—and the truth behind her actions—is their responsibility, Rhea, not ours.'

'Maybe she's in love; maybe it's nothing more than that.'

'You could be right, so do what you can and try to get co-operation from that fairground staff The fact you're asking about a missing girl might persuade them to co-operate.'

Off I went carrying the description of Kay. As I drove along the eight miles or so to Brantsford my mind was upon how I should best approach this enquiry. I did not want to antagonize the fairground people with a veiled accusation that they might have abducted the girl, but at the same time I did not want them to conceal her presence if she was living with them. If she was capable of appearing to be older than her true age, then one of the workers might have been fooled by her appearance and demeanour and might have taken her into his caravan with a view to her remaining with him. Whatever lay ahead, I knew I must handle this enquiry with considerable tact and delicacy. One problem was that no single person was in overall charge of the travelling fair. There was no boss, so no one accepted total responsibility for its members, which meant I would have to ask the same questions from the workers and the occupants of caravans.

It dawned upon me that some members of the crew might be unaware of the behaviour of just one of their colleagues. After all, they were a disparate group of individuals travelling together with a single aim. It was not a single organization on the move.

Filey was a busy but small seaside resort and with so many people milling around while the fair was up and running there on its temporary site, it would have been easy for a girl to slip unobserved into one of the caravans. That would be especially the case under cover of darkness, although darkness came very late on the summer feast day of Saints Gervase and Protase.

At this stage I had no power to search the vehicles for her so I would have to rely on the goodwill of the travellers themselves and they would all support one another, especially against inquisitiveness by the police. It might not be an easy enquiry.

Kay had disappeared on Friday evening after school—probably during daylight hours. Because Filey was not too far away from her home in Strensford, albeit in a different county, she could have joined the fair on that Friday night. There were regular buses along the coast from her home in Strensford to Filey, and the trip would have taken her less than an hour. On the Saturday she could have concealed herself in one of the caravans, clearly with the consent of its usual occupant. It was quite feasible that she could have then travelled with the fair to its new destination on Sunday.

Now I began to wonder when her parents had actually reported her absence. Had they delayed making the report for some reason? Had enquiries been made of the fairground personnel when they were in Filey over the weekend? By Monday most, if not all, the components of the fair would be in Brantsford some thirty miles inland. The fair was a real triumph of organization, military-like in its execution and precision, but was it sufficiently self-contained and isolated from the community to conceal a runaway girl? I thought it was. I felt she could have safely hidden herself while in Filey, but, inevitably, there would be a time when she would have to emerge. I figured that once the fair was stationary in Brantsford, Kay would surely want to leave the caravan occasionally. She might want to do some grocery shopping for her new friend or friends, to visit the ladies' toilets in town, help with the work of preparing the fair for its stay, or even to purchase some cosmetics or fresh underwear she might have forgotten to take with her. She did have some money of her own, £25 according to the circular.

As I pondered the case during my drive, I thought it unlikely she would remain out of sight for the whole time. There was a faint possibility she might have bought a post-card to send to her parents to assure them she was safe, or she may have gone to a telephone kiosk to ring them, if they had a phone. In the circumstances as we knew them, those actions were barely feasible—but not impossible.

If she had briefly left the shelter of the fairground's vehi-cles, Kay could have been noticed by someone in this small town—the shops were shut on Sunday, her day of arrival. Monday—yesterday—could have witnessed her first venture outside. Certainly the town was small enough for a stranger to be noticed, particularly if she was associated with the fair. That provided my first point of enquiry: I would ask around the shops, most of which were clustered around the mar-ket-place close to the fairground vehicles. I hoped my tour of those premises might be noticed by some of the fairground workers. If I were spotted before I got around to quizzing them, it would not appear as if I was concentrating on them, or accusing them of anything. I could stress they were merely part of my ongoing enquiries because they happened to be in town at this particular time.

Having determined my strategy, I arrived in Brantsford to find the streets and market-place almost deserted, except for the fairground vehicles, rides and stalls, none of which was open or functioning. It was not yet 9.30 and, apart from the fact that one would not expect fairground customers at this time of the morning, some of the equipment was under-going safety tests and routine maintenance. Consequently the workers were buzzing around like bees, dealing with the necessary work. I was pleased to see how conscientious and careful they were—nothing was left to chance.

I parked my motor bike on a patch of tarmac close to the town hall—the market-place extended only some 200 yards in either direction from it—and so began my tour of the shops. I was armed with my photograph and description of Kay and almost immediately sensed that my arrival had caused interest among the busy fairground workers. I was aware of a cessation in their chatter as they noticed me going about my enquiries around the shops and there was no doubt I had generated some curiosity among them. As I moved around the town, I took great care not to show any particular interest in the fair, making a point of calling in shops that I thought Kay might have visited. Despite my efforts, however, I learned nothing of interest. When my perambulations took me very close to the fairground vehicles, I looked out for Kay among the busy men, women and even children at work upon their vehicles, but did not see anyone resembling her. Her fair hair would have been very prominent among so many people with black hair.

My tour of the shops took about an hour; I had to accept this was early on a Tuesday morning when most people would not yet have ventured out shopping, but in every case, the shopkeepers promised to ring Ashfordly Police Station if they spotted anyone resembling her. I did not suggest she might have run away with the fairground workers—my tactic was to suggest she might have come to Brantsford for reasons no one knew. As I progressed around the shops, I realized it would be necessary to repeat the task later when the town was busier.

That's when Kay would probably emerge so that she was relatively anonymous among the crowds. So had I arrived too early for my visit to be beneficial? I thought not because I knew I had succeeded in creating interest in the girl's whereabouts although a follow-up visit would be sensible.

And all the time I was calling at the shops, I knew the eyes of the fairground workers were following my progress, doubtless very curious about the reason for my presence. Rather like a fly-fisherman uses a realistic image to tempt a trout, I knew I had attracted their interest—did they think

I was gathering complaints about them? I hoped that was what they were thinking because when I did ask my questions about Kay, they might hopefully show a sense of relief that they were not my targets.

Now it was time to put my theory to the test. Standing near one of the merry-go-rounds currently in the final stages of construction was a large woman with a swarthy complexion and a mass of jet-black hair. She'd be in her sixties, I estimated, and I knew she had been following my progression with some curiosity. I walked across to her with the leaflet in my hand.

'Good morning, I wonder if you can help me?'

'We're not in bother are we? Parking here?' and I noticed a cheeky glint in her eyes. 'And we've not thrown our rubbish into the street.'

'No,' I assured her. 'No problem.' Then for good measure, I added, 'It's good to see you all here, the town needs an attraction like this.'

'It's not often I hear a copper say we're welcome, they usually want rid of us . . .'

'Not around here we don't! So, can you help me with an enquiry?'

'Depends.'

'It's a young girl who's missing; her parents think she might be somewhere in Brantsford so I'm alerting all the shops. This is a photo of her; she's fifteen but nearly sixteen, and often looks older when she's dressed up and made-up.'

She took the photo and squinted at it as she drew it close to her face; it seemed she required spectacles.

'I can see long distance no problem.' She smiled that cheeky grin again. 'But, yes, I've seen her.'

'You have?' I couldn't believe this. 'Here, was she?'

'No, at Filey. We were there last week. I saw her on Friday before we packed up to come here. She was with a chap who used to work with us; he helped to look after the dodgems but on that Friday he said he had to be moving on. He said he thought we might be travelling further afield, not just heading the few miles over here to Brantsford. When he knew we were coming here, he said he wanted to move further away, not tie himself down to this part of the world. He left before we closed for the night so he wasn't with us on Saturday or Sunday, and he's not with us now. And neither is she, if that's what you're going to ask.'

'Any idea where he might be?'

'He said he was going to try his luck with the fairs in and around Hull for starters, but that big fair isn't until October. He might have found one there he could join for a while, and some of them do move around the country, down south and into the West Country.'

'Devon and Cornwall? As far as that?'

'Some like to try other places; we tend to stay around the north.' She was surprisingly chatty. 'Anyway, that chap walked away from us with a rucksack of belongings on his back and his week's wages in his pocket, and the girl went with him. It almost seemed as if it had all been planned, she meeting him just when he was leaving.'

'It does look rather like that.'

'I'm a mum, Mister Policeman, and I don't hold with older men like him cavorting with under-age girls, but she did look more than fifteen or sixteen, I must say. I know some girls are like flies around a midden when the fair comes to town, but we're not like that. We're good people, Mr Policeman. Rough mebbe, but honest, and not ones for getting young lasses into trouble. So there you are. He's your man.'

'An older man, you say? Any idea how old?'

'Hard to say for an old woman like me, but I'd put him in his middle thirties, too old for a kid like her. But girls do like older men with experience and money, men who have done exciting things.'

'Thanks, that's a wonderful help. Do you know his name? Or anything else about him?'

'He called himself Danny when he was with us. Nothing else, just Danny. We don't pry, you see, we take people on face value. I've no idea where he came from; he just turned up last week when we were in Filey saying he was looking for temporary work.'

'It happens a lot does it, in your profession?'

'Oh yes, we get all sorts of people seeking work with us, usually on a very short-term basis. We said he could help run the dodgems, then we might find something else for him to do, depending on any skills he might have. There's always repairs to be made, safety checks to make, and so on.'

'And was he capable of that? Running the dodgems?'

'Oh yes, he was capable of better things. He was a good, honest worker when he put his mind to it, but he oozed with charm when girls were around. I wouldn't trust any young girl in his clutches.'

'Did he step out of order? Do anything to any of your girls?'

'No, he wouldn't have remained long if he had! It might have been all talk, the way he dealt with the girls and young women. Some men are like that, all talk!' and she grinned at me cheekily.

'Can you describe him?'

'I didn't take too much notice while he was here, but he was a tall chap with dark hair, six foot I'd say, but very slender and handsome, utterly charming, a real lady killer if ever there was one.'

'Did he have transport?'

'A fairly smart car, dark blue, medium size. Not too big and flashy and not too small. Don't ask me what sort it was, I've no idea.'

I asked a few more questions just to test her knowledge, but I realized she had told me everything she knew. When I suggested talking to other members of the group, she shook her head.

'No point, Mr Policeman, they'll not talk to you. I do the talking and if I don't tell you, no one else will.'

'So I am lucky this morning?'

'Just because it's a young lass you're concerned about, and because the chap concerned has left us. We want to help her, but we owe him nothing.'

'Thanks, you've been very helpful, I appreciate it.'

'We can be helpful when it's needed and if we're treated right.'

'Thanks, I'll remember that. I'll get onto this straight away. Just a couple of points before I go. Did you tell the police in Filey that you'd seen that girl? Or, more to the point, did they ask if you'd seen her before you left the area?'

'No. No one asked us and I didn't report it. We had no police asking questions in Filey. I mean, she did look more than sixteen so her love affair is nowt to do with me and neither of 'em was breaking the law so far as I knew. The way they reacted to each other when I saw 'em made me think they knew one another fairly well and I told you I thought they'd arranged that meeting. They weren't strangers, if you know what I mean.'

'And she didn't join you? Stay overnight even on that Friday?'

'Not her—she went off with him. She never spent any time with us at all. I've never seen her since.'

'Thanks again.'

'Let me know how you get on, Mr Policeman, I'd be interested.'

'That's a promise.' And I left her.

I hurried back to the office in Ashfordly where Sergeant Blaketon was chatting to PC Alf Ventress about a crime prevention campaign soon to be launched in Ashfordly. As I walked in, Blaketon said, 'Ah, Rhea. You look excited!'

'I've got some good news,' and I explained in detail the outcome of my visit to Brantsford.

'That's great. Congratulations. But you can't go dashing off to Hull to go looking for them, it's not in our patch and neither is Filey. Hull's big fair isn't until the autumn, so you'd better contact Strensford Police and pass the information on to them, get them to check whether there are any small fairs in Hull in the meantime. It's their case, not ours, so it's up to them to see it through. Don't you get involved in their work.'

And so I did exactly as he had instructed and resumed my patrol in and around Aidensfield, hoping I would be informed of any further news about the missing girl.

As I had been very much on the fringes of that enquiry, I knew nothing of the background to the case, nothing about Kay Goodwin's home conditions, nothing about her parents, nor indeed anything about her school life or recreational habits. Somehow, I felt it would have helped to find her if I had known more about the girl and her home situation, but I told myself it was nothing to do with me. I had done my bit because I had quickly managed to trace the fair thought to have been the one she had run away to join. Although she had not joined the fair currently operating in Brantsford, I had produced a valuable piece of evidence by establishing she had probably gone to Hull with a man called Danny who was a lot older than her. Short of searching every fairground vehicle in Brantsford, I was now confident she was not travelling with that fair. I sensed the woman had been honest with me. I had fulfilled my duty and should have been satisfied with the outcome of my efforts, but for some inexplicable reason I wasn't. There was an unexplained void, but I couldn't identify precisely what it was but it was the sole responsibility of Strensford Police to find her, not mine.

It was while trying to put the Kay Goodwin enquiry to the back of my mind that, quite suddenly during a quiet patrol, I recognized the void that had been troubling me. It was simply this: there had been nothing in the newspapers or on the television or radio news about the missing schoolgirl. I thought that was quite odd. Having been reared in a village not far from Strensford, I received the local weekly, *The Strensford Gazette*, in addition to the regional *Yorkshire Post* and *Northern Echo* but none had carried any news of Kay's disappearance. Similarly, neither the BBC or ITV regional TV news programmes, or any of the radio news bulletins had made reference to the case—I would have known because I took great care to listen to them all in case they broadcast anything associated with my duties. Missing persons were often featured, particularly if they were vulnerable like the old or infirm, or if they were very young children, the right kind of publicity could help in tracing them. In my view, the unexplained disappearance of a fifteen-year-old girl warranted wide publicity, not only locally but on a national scale. After all, people could travel great distances quickly by train and car. Even though a school friend had thought she was running away to join a travelling fair, that did not fully explain her actions—no reason had been given for her behaviour—and she had *not* joined a fair, certainly not the one that had been in Filey. So had she now joined another fair with Danny?

It occurred to me that she would not have made the decision to run away without a very strong reason. As I brooded over the case I felt there were several puzzling aspects of Kay's disappearance, and I was certain it justified positive publicity, but there had been nothing other than a short note in an internal police circular. And, of course, that was confidential and not for the eyes of the press or public. Kay had left home on Friday ostensibly to join a fair but from what the fairground woman had told me, no police had made enquiries at that particular fair. So where was Kay now? Clearly she had not returned home otherwise I would have known. And who was the man? I needed to discuss my concerns with someone and Mary was my first choice.

Over our evening meal that night, and with the children safely in bed, I aired my worries and she listened with her customary patience. Then she said, 'Nick, I can appreciate your concern, but it's not your case. You mustn't interfere. If there has been no publicity, then that will have been a carefully considered decision by Strensford Police for reasons you may never know.'

'But it doesn't make sense . . .'

'To be frank, Nick, it's nothing to do with you now; you've done your bit so I can't understand why you're getting yourself so involved with it.'

'It's just that everything about this enquiry seems to have been so casual and lacking real impact—even the note in our

Crime Information Sheet didn't suggest there was any undue concern about her. She must be at risk; she's only fifteen.'

'There's bound to be concern, Nick, her family will be distraught.'

'You'd think so. So why haven't they alerted the newspapers?'

'Possibly because the local police advised them not to.'

'But why would they do that? You'd think the local police—and the girl's parents—would want all the help they can get from a wave of publicity. There are no better hunters and searchers than members of the public out and about with their eyes wide open. Thousands of people on the look-out are infinitely more useful than a scattering of policemen with lots of other things to concern them.'

'I appreciate all that, Nick, but you know and I know that there are times when no publicity is the wisest course of action for all sorts of reasons that usually remain secret. Can't you just accept that might be the situation here?'

She was right of course. There must be a sound reason why the case had not been publicized and, as I kept telling myself, it was nothing to do with me. The answer to my riddle could only be that there were hidden factors involved in Kay's disappearance that must be kept out of the public domain. I could not think what they might be—on the face of it, this was nothing more than a fairly common case of a teenage girl running away from home.

In the momentary silence that followed our chat, I continued to brood over the affair when Mary said, 'If you're not happy, have words with Sergeant Blaketon. I can't see what else you can do.'

'I know what he'll say! He'll tell me "Leave it alone, Rhea, you've done your bit".'

'Exactly. Everything that can be done is being done.'

'Am I being daft, Mary? Banging on like this about something over which I have no control? And in which I have no further involvement?'

'I know you take your work very seriously, but I think there's nothing more you can do. What else can I say?'

'Right,' was all I could think of by way of response. But I continued to think there were many unanswered questions. After a few days, of course, my concern began to subside as other duties came along to keep me fully occupied.

Then, by chance, a few days later I had to telephone Strensford Police to ask that an officer be allowed to interview a witness to a road traffic accident on my Aidensfield beat. Two cars had collided on the Aidensfield-Elsinby road and a witness had stopped at the scene to help. He had handed his name and address to one of the drivers. The witness lived in Strensford and I needed his version of events before I submitted my Form 96, the document used to record a traffic accident. When I rang, the phone was answered by PC Chris Langley who had been a colleague of mine on our initial training course. After chatting about old times, I gave the reason for my call and he said he would personally interview my witness and send the material to me via the force's internal mail. I thanked him, and then, when he asked if I was enjoying my work and if I was kept busy, I decided to ask about any progress in the search for Kay Goodwin. After all, her home was in Strensford so, as a local police officer, he would be aware of the enquiries. I explained my involvement without expressing my personal concerns, but asked whether Kay had been traced.

'Not a sign of them,' he said. 'Vanished into thin air, like a cloud of smoke.'

'Them?' I queried.

'Kay and her dad,' said Chris.

'Her dad? I had no idea he was being sought.'

'We think they've run away together, Nick. We don't think Kay is in any danger, but we want to trace them, him especially.'

'I just thought we were looking for her,' I told him. 'That's the message we got. I found the Filey travelling fair in Brantsford, but the girl hadn't joined them, as one of her school-friends had indicated.'

'Right, we know that. We got your message that she wasn't with that fair. But by the time we were told of the girl's disappearance, the fair had left Filey and no one knew where it was heading. We thought she had joined it, hence that circular, we wanted every travelling fair in the region to be traced and checked.'

'You know a good deal about it, Chris.'

'I got the first report; I've been involved from the start. Kay's mother didn't report her absence until the Sunday as she thought the girl had gone to stay with a school-friend for the weekend. Kay told her mum she and her friend were hoping to go to the fair so her mum wasn't concerned when she didn't come home from school. Kay has often done that, gone to stay with that friend for the weekend. It was only when the father vanished as well that the mother became concerned and told us, and now we think they are both together somewhere.'

'Did you get my full message from Brantsford?'

'You confirmed Kay had been seen in Filey on the Friday evening, but that she wasn't with the fair in Brantsford. Yes, we got that.'

'What about the rest of it? That she was with a man who was older than herself?'

'No, I didn't get that part of it!'

'Well, I passed on the information that she'd been seen with an older man at Filey on the Friday. A tall handsome man, dark-haired, about thirty-five, driving a dark-coloured car of some sort and that they were heading for a travelling fair based in Hull. That was all part of my message to your office.'

'Hull? That information never reached me, Nick. The only stuff I got passed to me was that Kay was not with that fair that had been in Filey!'

'This is one of the problems of a case not being followed right the way through by one officer. Messages never get passed along in their entirety, so much valuable information is ignored,' I grumbled. 'And another thing, I was surprised there was no publicity about her.'

'She was thought to be with her dad, Nick, and he was wanted for questioning about alleged false accounting in the Finance Department of Strensford Rural District council offices. That's where he worked. He knew the balloon was about to go up when the auditors were called in, so he packed his bags and cleared off. We didn't court publicity in case he went to ground somewhere. We wanted him to be unaware of the hunt for him.'

'*I* was unaware of the hunt for him! I was just looking for Kay!'

'I didn't draft the original message, Nick. I'm only a small cog in a fairly large wheel. Anyway, after dad had cleared off, Kay ran away; she didn't stay with her friend. We thought Kay and her dad might be together because she adored him. He was a handsome chap . . .'

'So is he about thirty-five years old, six feet tall, dark-haired and handsome?' I said, thinking of the information I had received and despatched.

'That sounds like him, Nick.'

'Then he's the man I told your people about. The man she met at Filey. He'd worked with the fair on the dodgems before leaving that Friday, that's when his daughter met up with him. I told your office about that, Chris; I'm appalled the information hasn't got to where it was needed.'

'Let's say there must have been a breakdown in communications, Nick. So what else did you find out?'

'That they were going to join a fair in Hull, but the big fair doesn't start there until October.'

'But big ships come into Hull and so do ferries and fishing boats. I think we'd better start asking around the docks and looking for his car. The father, whose name is Danny, got away with six thousand pounds from the council due to his swindle, so he won't be short of money and we know he took his passport when he vanished. He could be in Holland or anywhere in Europe. Why else would he go to Hull?'

'His daughter wouldn't need a passport, would she? If she was under sixteen?'

'Right, Nick. I'm sorry about this, but if I get involved in this enquiry all over again, I might not have time to interview your traffic-accident witness! But I will make sure someone does—and that they get things right. But thanks for this, Nick. Glad you called. I'll get onto CID immediately.'

The runaways were traced to Holland where Daniel Goodwin had found work with a Dutch engineering company that had factories in England, so his English language and his knowledge of accounting would be very useful.

And Kay had also got work in the same company, each on the proviso that the necessary documents would eventually be forwarded from England. Chris Langley later told me the CID had decided to call in Interpol in order to complete the case and to try and secure extradition of the couple.

As things transpired, the pair returned home because they could not remain in Holland due to a lack of the necessary paperwork and their true details becoming known through the police liaison between Holland and the UK. Daniel decided to return home to confront his accusers and was later given a three-year prison sentence, suspended for two years, chiefly because he repaid most of the money. The reason for his attempt to defraud his employers was never known. Kay did not continue her education. She left school when she was sixteen and obtained work in an hotel in Strensford, as a trainee receptionist.

And throughout it all, the case attracted absolutely no publicity, except for Daniel Goodwin's sentence for his fraudulent actions.

I couldn't thank my lady contact who had acted as the fair's spokesperson because by the time all this had become known to me, the funfair and its complement of workers had left Brantsford for an unknown destination.

Maybe they would return next year when I could thank my fair lady.

4. SCARBOROUGH FAIR

During my early years as the constable of Aidensfield, I had very little professional contact with officers based at Scarborough Police Station simply because my beat was not situated within Scarborough Division. It was true, however, that some of my local enquiries necessitated officers in Scarborough making enquiries on my behalf, but I was never called upon to undertake tours of duty in that famous and historic seaside spa town, known to many as The Queen of Watering Places.

In later years, the boundary changes that affected every police force in England and Wales firstly in 1968 and later in 1974 meant that Ashfordly and the rural beats within its sectional boundaries became part of Scarborough Division. My earlier divisional headquarters at Malton was absorbed and had to have its status reduced to that of a sub-division. The seaside towns of Whitby and Strensford also became part of the massive Scarborough Division that became known in police terminology as 'D' Division. In 1974 the new county of North Yorkshire—the largest in England despite being only part of the whole Yorkshire—comprised four huge police divisions, all measured in area rather than population. They were 'A' Division (York); 'B' Division (Harrogate),

'C' Division (Richmond) and 'D' Division (Scarborough). There was also a road traffic division known as 'T' Division. The territory within 'D' Division included a long stretch of the Yorkshire coast and that division alone extended more than thirty miles inland. However, most of those changes occurred after I had left Aidensfield.

Nonetheless, while on patrol within my own beat of Aidensfield, or perhaps undertaking shifts in Ashfordly, I would often be accosted by tourists and holidaymakers looking for Whitby, Scarborough and Strensford, as well as the coastal villages of Robin Hood's Bay, Runswick Bay and Staithes. I was surprised how many hadn't brought maps with them and did not know the way to Scarborough even though that was their destination! Not content with asking the way, they also wanted me to recommend sights, locations and good places to eat or drink.

Some thought Scarborough was in the East Riding of Yorkshire (it was then in the North Riding but is now within a new county known as North Yorkshire). And I had even encountered travel writers who wrote that it was situated on the west coast of England or even in East Anglia. One tourist thought it was in Scotland and another felt it was somehow linked with Blackpool. People living in the South of England really didn't have a clue, although some thought it might be somewhere up north near Birmingham or Liverpool because they were 'north'. I once received a letter addressed to me at York Police Station with the address shown as 'York Police, York, Lancashire'. It came from Chelmsford.

Scarborough is an historic coastal town and port dating to Roman times and other early invaders such as the Saxons and Normans played their part in its long and interesting development. Its magnificent castle, once thought impregnable, overlooks Scarborough's two fine bays while a little-known area close to the seafront comprises fascinating old streets that are reminiscent of York and Chester. Its old houses include one where Richard III is said to have lodged, and the Three Mariners Inn that is more than 650 years old.

Many tourists never visit that part of the old town, preferring the seafront with its candy floss, seafood and amusement arcades.

Scarborough is renowned as England's first seaside resort due to the discovery *c.*1620 of its health-giving mineral waters. They were found by a Mrs Farrow when a spring, then called a spaw, appeared near the site of the present spa buildings.

It was much later that the advent of the railway system brought millions of visitors to Scarborough to 'take the waters'. They believed that the mineral water from that spring would make them healthier and cure most of their ailments. Later, private cars helped to swell tourist numbers and happily Scarborough with its splendid seafront and beaches has sufficient interesting sights and locations to cater for most tastes, and to accommodate its many and varied admirers from Britain and overseas. With Scarborough less than an hour's drive from my Aidensfield beat, one of the regular questions I was asked by holidaymakers and day-trippers was 'When and where is Scarborough Fair?'

The question arose due to the popularity of the song made famous by Paul Simon and Art Garfunkel in 1966. It was on their album entitled *Parsley, Sage, Rosemary and Thyme* and was called 'Scarborough Fair'. The first of its ten verses was:

Are you going to Scarborough Fair?
Parsley, sage, rosemary and thyme
Remember me to one who lives there,
For she once was a true love of mine.

The narrator of this traditional folk song, which is said to date from medieval times, was a man who had been rejected by the girl he considered to be his true love. In the song, he appears to be asking travellers who are heading for Scarborough Fair to find the girl and ask her to complete a series of difficult or impossible tasks by which she will show that she truly loves the jilted character. For example, he asks her to plough the land with the horn of a lamb and reap it with a sickle of leather, or to make him a shirt without any seams or fine needlework.

The name of the composer is not known because in medieval times, people called bards or minstrels would sing the words as they travelled from town to town, and thereafter others would recall the verses and repeat them at future events, often changing the words to suit their own purposes. The interpretation and precise wording of 'Scarborough Fair' therefore will almost certainly have changed over the centuries. It is not known why Scarborough is specifically mentioned, but the reference to herbs, i.e., parsley, sage, rosemary and thyme, is probably because medieval people used them to symbolize love or desire in much the same way that modern lovers use red roses.

Following the success of the 1966 revival of the song, people took an increased interest in Scarborough's association with the famous fair. Their questions became more frequent as the song was repeated time and time again, most of them wondering when the fair was open, where it was held, and how they could get there.

To familiarize myself with the fair's history, I decided to do a little research and discovered that Scarborough Fair had ended in 1788. It had been an enduring and busy fair, created by royal charter in 1253. It differed from others because it continued for forty-five days, an exceptionally long period even by standards of that time, and its stallholders came from afar, including dozens from overseas. At the time, Scarborough was noted as an international port with a variety of commodities being traded through its harbour and docks, and so the huge fair included produce and goods from all over the world.

However, drunkenness, bad behaviour and general lawlessness became a feature of the event and this, coupled with a decline of Scarborough as a major port, resulted in the demise of the original Scarborough Fair in 1788.

In more recent times, attempts have been made to revive it, albeit not in its original gigantic forty-five day form, although types of continental fairs have since been held there. The truth is, of course, that Scarborough Fair has become more of a legend than a reality and that was certainly enhanced by the enormous popularity of Simon and Garfunkel's haunting song. Once I had established those facts in my mind, I could reliably inform anyone of the true history of the fair and such enquiries continued for several years both of me and other police officers. In most modern minds, though, Scarborough Fair is little more than an ancient myth whose appeal lies in that popular song.

However, two strange things occurred on Aidensfield beat that reminded me of the real Scarborough Fair and they caused me to consider its impact on the local people all those centuries ago.

The first was the discovery of some ancient silver coins on the moors. In medieval times, there was a network of tracks, paths and stone-paved trods that criss-crossed the moors to link the main centres of population. A number of them led eventually to the coast and to major towns and cities like York, Hull and Scarborough. Some routes were patronized chiefly by pilgrims and monks as they moved between the abbeys that abounded within and near the moors, while others were busy with long trains of pack-horses carrying their loads across those desolate heights. Beside some of the paths were simple structures of stone, often without a roof, which provided a small degree of shelter from the ever-present winds and were welcomed both by travelling humans and the resident moorland sheep. They still exist and are known as bields, being sufficiently substantial to feature on large-scale maps. A bield is a dry stone wall some three or four feet high (90 to 120 cm) and perhaps ten yards long (9m or so); it is sometimes constructed with a short angled extension at each end. It does not have a roof and its purpose is to protect the animals from the wind; bields are carefully sited to give maximum protection. Quite often, they are utilized by hikers if a sudden storm erupts or if they merely want a short rest from persistent moorland winds.

In my time at Aidensfield, most of the moorland tracks had disappeared through lack of use, as new roads had been constructed to cater for motor vehicles, although some evidence of the old routes could still be seen and their routes plotted. Lots of ramblers and historians, archaeologists, ornithologists and naturalists of all persuasions made good use of those old routes, sometimes finding hidden paving stones beneath the thick coating of heather. Lots of the old paths and highways though have disappeared forever, some of them beneath modern roads.

It was while parked on a lofty site in the moors above Aidensfield in my official Mini-van with its blue light and *POLICE* logo that I saw a hiker approaching from across the moor. He wore sturdy hiking clothes and carried a rucksack on his back; he was also carrying what looked like a mine detector. I was updating my pocket book at the time and managed to complete my entry as I realized the man was heading towards me, evidently wanting to make contact. I climbed out and awaited his arrival, looking out across the vast treeless emptiness that typifies much of the North York Moors. It was a warm, dry and sunny day in May, and I was enjoying my patrol of those remote places.

My chosen point provided spectacular views across the dales below and was often used by visitors who paused for a picnic or merely to admire the view. It was known as Hagstone Rigg and the unofficial parking area was located beside a minor unclassified road. At that point the road crossed an ancient trod that was now used only by ramblers. Centuries ago, this had probably been a major crossroads.

'Good afternoon, Officer.' The oncoming man was about fifty years of age, I guessed, a thin character with lots of grey hair including a beard and moustache. His sharp face was weathered by regular exposure to the open air and his eyes were noticeably blue. His clothing was ideal for exploring the remote areas while his boots looked creased and comfortable but well maintained. He had a map protected from rain by a clear plastic cover hanging around his neck. As he stopped, he placed his mine detector on the ground.

'Hello,' I greeted him. 'A grand day and a nice view.'

'And we're both lucky enough to be able to enjoy it all,' he smiled. 'There are many less fortunate than ourselves.'

'And I'm getting paid for being here!' I joked. 'All part of my routine duty. As you say, some of us are lucky.'

'Talking of luck'—he swung his rucksack from his back and stood it on the ground beside his detector—'I thought you'd better see these, I found them along my route not long ago.'

He began to open the straps of a side pocket.

'I was going to take them into Strensford Police Station, but it's a bit out of my way, so perhaps you can advise me on the correct procedure. Do I really have to report this discovery? I know I don't have to report found pottery or things made from iron, copper or bronze, but these are coins and I think they're silver.'

Having opened the side pocket, he reached in to extract a handful of small dirty coins that he passed to me. I took them and studied them, but they were very dirty and any markings on them were far from clear. I counted them. There were fourteen, all seemingly identical.

'What are they? Have you any idea?' I asked.

'It's hard to tell due to the dirt, but I think they are pennies from the reign of Henry VII.' He took one from me, leaving the others in my hand to examine as he spoke. 'If you look closely you can just see the image of a king sitting on a throne. That being so, these are known as sovereign pennies and they date from the period around 1480 to 1500.'

'Really? Where did you find them?'

'Beside this footpath, about four or five miles that way,' and he indicated to the east. 'I've got this detector; it's an old army mine detector that I bought from the Army and Navy Stores some years ago, but it's most useful for locating hidden treasure like this. I go on long walks on known medieval routes and scan the paths as I go—it's amazing how many coins, buckles and knives can be found beside these old paths and trods.'

'Were they all together? In a jar, or perhaps a bag of some kind,' I asked, thinking of the rules that governed the finding of treasure trove.

'No, these were spread out at intervals along the side of the path, one every half-mile or so. All on the same side of the path, the right-hand side.'

'So how do we account for them being there?'

'I might be using too much imagination, but I wondered if it was a trader of some kind, walking along this route all those years ago with a hole in his pocket, or in his satchel, or whatever he was carrying his coins in. And they could have fallen out, one by one, with the movement of his body, at regular intervals.'

'You could be right, so what made you think of that?'

'This old path was one of the ancient pannier routes sometimes known as causeys. Traders would use trains of pack-horses to cross the moors with their loads as they travelled to and from markets and fairs, or even down to the coast to catch a ship for their produce. This particular route goes to Scarborough and dates to the time of Scarborough Fair; it's part of a network of old causeys that merged as they drew nearer to the coast.'

'Scarborough Fair ended in 1788'—I aired my recently discovered knowledge—'but it was very busy in its heyday.'

'It was. It attracted traders from far and wide, both from over the sea and here inland, hence this network of causeys. That is why I think these coins were lost by a trader either on his way to or from Scarborough Fair.'

'Well, the first thing you need to know is that there is no obligation upon you to report finding things made of stone, china, glass, copper, bronze and most other things. You know that, as you have told me. However, if you find objects made of either silver or gold, or containing silver or gold as many coins do, then they have to be reported to the coroner so that he can hold an inquest into the discovery. Inquest is an old word for a coroner's enquiry. Objects made of precious stone don't have to be reported—unless they contain silver or gold. Silver and gold are the key factors.'

'I thought that was the case and I know there is some kind of formality involved. So do I have to report these?'

'Treasure trove belongs to the state.' I felt he should be aware of some more details. 'The purpose of the inquest is to decide whether found gold or silver is treasure trove, and that depends upon where and how it was found. The crux of the matter is whether it was *originally hidden*. People used to hide gold and silver coins or other goods to prevent the state getting their hands on them as a form of tax. The logic behind the treasure trove system is that the state still gets its tax, even centuries later! So, if the coroner decides your find was silver or gold and that it had been deliberately concealed all those years ago, he will declare it treasure trove. That means it goes to the state but you will get the market value for it—and the trove will go to a museum.'

'So it pays to be honest if you find it nowadays.'

'Indeed it does; if you don't report found gold or silver to the coroner, it could be confiscated.'

'But these coins were surely lost.'

'That would seem to be the case,' I agreed. 'But if they are silver, then you should report your discovery, just to be on the safe side. That is done through the police. The inquest will follow eventually and in your case, the coroner will probably agree they were lost and so they will be returned to you, even if they are made of silver or gold. The coroner does not determine ownership of silver or gold found on private property, having been originally lost. That is a matter for the landowner and finder to sort out for themselves.'

'Well, I'll donate them to the museum nearest to the place I found them!'

'That should make everyone happy. Perhaps I should add that the coroner doesn't establish their value even if they are declared treasure trove; that is done by independent experts.'

'I follow, so can I report these to you? As my form of safeguard?'

'You can, but I would need to give you an official receipt which I don't have with me, but I can get one from Ashfordly Police Station. You can either make your own way there to report them to the duty officer, or I can take you now, in my van. And if you wish to continue your journey from here, I can bring you back, or take you on somewhere else. But if you do report the coins to me now, it means you don't risk losing them all over again.'

And so he agreed. I obtained his name, full address and telephone number—his name was George Moore and he lived in Leeds—and I drove him to Ashfordly along with his rucksack and mine detector. PC Alf Ventress was on duty in Ashfordly Police Station. He took particulars and issued Mr Moore with a receipt for the coins, saying we would have them examined by experts to establish whether they contained any silver before deciding whether or not to inform the coroner.

When the procedures were complete, Mr Moore said he would appreciate being returned to the point I had collected him and so I obliged, promising to keep in touch about his coins. I took them to a jeweller in Ashfordly who carefully examined them and declared they did contain a high proportion of silver, so I was obliged to notify the coroner. He held inquests into such discoveries once every three months—quite a lot of buried treasure was found in and around the moors—and so we had to wait until his next sitting. Once we had some expert analysis of the coins, I asked Leeds City Police to obtain a written statement from Mr Moore to outline his discovery with precise dates, times and places and this was placed before HM Coroner prior to the inquest.

As expected, he decided that although the coins contained silver, they should not be declared treasure trove because it was evident they had not been deliberately concealed. He thought they had probably been lost by a traveller centuries ago on his moorland trek either to or from Scarborough and its fair. The coins were returned to Mr Moore who donated them to the Rotunda Museum in Scarborough.

In the days and weeks that followed, I frequently parked for a few quiet moments on that isolated moorland site at Hagstone Rigg. It was a peaceful place and conducive to creative thinking and when I was there I would update my notebook and plan my route for the day's duty. Often when I was there I tried, not very successfully, to visualize the lives of those who trudged across those bleak heights while heading for Scarborough Fair.

I thought too about the man in the folk song who had lost the love of his life and who might have been one of those travellers who was trying to find her, or get a message to her at Scarborough Fair—indeed, he could have been the very one who had lost those coins. But the chances of that happening were astronomical.

When a body was discovered very close to those same moors a few months later, I found I could not forget Scarborough Fair. Human remains and artefacts buried in graves for the deceased's final journey to Heaven were regularly found on the moors, many dating from ancient times, such as the Stone Age, Bronze Age and even the Romans. Old records contain accounts of human bones being found on the more remote parts of the moors above Rosedale, Glaisdale and Goathland. Many of them had not been buried and were the mortal remains of people who had perished either in severe weather conditions, or simply through getting lost in that lofty and windswept wilderness. One such story concerns a cork seller who trekked across the moors selling his wares to innkeepers. During the nineteenth century he got lost in a ferocious snowstorm near an old inn at Hamer between Glaisdale and Rosedale. He had been heading for the inn to sell some of his wares to the landlady, but had got lost in the dreadful snow and his skeletal remains were found some time afterwards. He was identified by the scattering of bottle corks around the bones and even as I compile these notes, small crosses or flowers can be seen in several lonely places on the moors. Invariably they mark the location of a lonely death many years ago. The identity of the people who continue to place the flowers or crosses at those remote sites is never revealed; they are one of the prevailing mysteries of that isolated area.

Human remains have also been discovered during operations that involved old buildings—on one occasion, the remains of a woman were found in an attic where she had apparently died many years earlier. The exact date of her death could not be determined. She was never identified and the occupants claimed they had no idea that there was a mummified body in their loft. They had never ventured into that part of the house; she was not a member of their family, and she remained unidentified.

In other cases, bodies had either been buried in long-forgotten graveyards or perhaps in fields and woodland. Even now, such discoveries are fairly commonplace in historic towns and villages—it is often said that property developers in York are almost afraid to excavate among the structures within the city walls for fear of what they might unearth—the origins of those walls date to the Romans. Most of those discoveries date from ancient times; nonetheless, each that involves human remains (or a hoard of gold or silver) must be investigated and the coroner must be informed.

A fairly common event on the moors occurred when ramblers found bones among the heather. In most cases they were the remains of a long-dead sheep whose skeletal parts had been bleached by long exposure to the weather and scattered by the activity of predators like foxes or kites. At times it was difficult to determine whether found bones, particularly something like a solitary rib, were human, or those of some other animal. A simple visual examination was not always guaranteed to provide an answer and so, if we received any such report, the bones were always examined by experts in laboratory conditions. For the police there were no problems if the bones were those of an animal. Even if they were human bones from the distant past, we took little official interest in them, except to arrange a decent burial in a local churchyard.

However, human remains from more recent times demanded careful attention from a scientific point of view as police officers, forensic scientists, pathologists and sometimes archaeologists did their best to determine the age and sex of the deceased and how death had occurred. So when what appeared to be a human skeleton was found on the moors within the area of my beat not far from where the Henry VII coins had been discovered, I had to establish an immediate enquiry.

The call came at lunchtime one Wednesday afternoon in June. By chance, I was in uniform but was at home having lunch before going out for a late tour of duty, i.e. from 2 p.m. until 10 p.m. When the phone rang in my office I thought it must be Sergeant Blaketon calling with specific instructions but it wasn't. It was a sheep farmer called Ned Lofthouse from Moorside Grange at Gelderslack on the moors above Ashfordly.

'Now then, Mr Rhea,' he spoke slowly and with great deliberation. 'Thoo'll 'ave ti come here sharpish, I've found summat nasty.'

'Really? What is it?'

'A corpse, Mr Rhea. A dead 'un. Very dead, I would say.'

'Human?'

'Aye. I shouldn't be ringing thoo if was a sheep or a cow.'

'Where is it?' was my next question.

'In a grave.'

'On your farm?'

'Nay, up on t'moors.'

'Who is it? Do you know?'

'No idea, Mr Rhea but if thoo asks me, I'd say he gat 'is time overed a few centuries ago, but thoo nivver can tell. Or it might be a she. Bones can seem ancient even after just a few weeks lying open to t'elements on our moors.'

'Right, I'll come straight away.'

'There's no great rush, he's not going to go anywhere, and I'm going to 'ave my dinner.'

And so it was that I drove out to Moorside Grange on its spectacular and lofty site above Gelderslack. Moorside Grange sounded rather grand, but it was merely a substantial stone-built farmhouse surrounded by sturdy outbuildings that protected it from the worst of the weather. It had been the family home for about 300 years with the main source of income being a large flock of blackfaced moorland sheep. Throughout the year, they survived on those desolate heights seemingly impervious to the weather. As I parked my motor bike in the foldyard, Ned came out to meet me.

'There's a mug o' tea in t'kitchen, Mr Rhea and our Jenny's got some of her fruit cake cut ready.'

I didn't like to say I had just had my lunch as this kind of hospitality was a feature of rural life in this region. So I left my helmet on the saddle of the bike and followed Ned indoors. He was a large, broad-shouldered man of about fifty with a ruddy complexion and a head of thick grey hair. He was dressed in the traditional corduroy trousers and checked shirt with its sleeves rolled up. I settled down at the kitchen table as Jenny, a small woman with a weathered face, poured me a mug of tea and passed me the piece of cake on a plate.

'Thanks, Jenny.'

'There's more where that came from, Mr Rhea, if you want it.'

'No thanks, this will be fine.'

Ned joined me and in a few minutes of silence, munched his own piece of cake as we prepared for our chat. I did not want to rush him—rushing was not the way of doing things here.

'It was summat of a surprise, Mr Rhea, I'll tell thoo that for nowt,' he began quite suddenly. I did not interrupt but let him tell the story in his own time.

'Digging, I was, with my digger, excavating some footings for a sheep bield. I'd just got started when t'digger shifted a big flat stone hidden under t'heather and blow me, there was other stones, smaller they were but covering these bones. When my digger moved the big 'un, it shifted some o' them little 'uns. Human bones they are—a skull an' ribs an' arms and legs an' things. Bits o' cloth an' all.'

'A grave you think? Or just a hollow in the moor?'

'Difficult to say, Mr Rhea. We do get barrows and howes up 'ere, burial grounds they were in times past, but not graves on their own, like I think this 'un is. But them stones covering it are a puzzle, eh?'

'They are. Who put them there? Is there an old burial ground nearby?'

'Nay, Mr Rhea, not that I know of. There's nowt to hint there's other bodies, bones and graves thereabouts. Not that I've looked for any more! And I left it just as it was, Mr Rhea, never touched a thing. Came straight in here to report it.'

'Good, that's exactly the right thing to do. So, Ned, let's go and have a look.'

'We'll take my tractor.'

We finished our cake and I stood on the rear platform of his tractor as we left the shelter of his buildings. We bumped along at a slow pace, not speaking due to the noise of the engine, and then he turned onto an unsurfaced moorland track that led to high ground to the north of his farm. After about ten minutes we crested a hillock and I could see his digger standing idle.

'Ovver yonder,' he shouted, above the noise of the engine.

He parked a short distance away and we walked to the scene.

'Down there,' he said, pointing to a hole in the ground.

I ventured close enough to peer into the hole without disturbing its edges. The big stone and several others, smaller but long enough to cover the grave's width, were beside the hole in the ground. It did not look like a coffin because there was no sign of woodwork or stonework beneath the stones that had been removed, although in the past, people were generally buried in wool or shrouds. The 'grave' comprised a shallow depression in the ground only some eighteen inches deep (45cm) and it was dry. Obviously, it was not a watercourse or drain. It was about two feet (60cm) wide and looked a natural hollow, not a man-made one. Lying in the hollow were the skeletal bones of a human being. I did not touch anything but merely stood in silence to absorb the scene and to record my impressions in my official notebook. Ned did not interrupt but stood a few yards away, patiently waiting.

I could discern a few tiny remnants of clothing, some leather from the shoes and a belt, some dark hair on the skull, and the fact that the covering stone had protected the remains from both the weather and any predators like foxes and birds. All the bones seemed to be there—they weren't scattered around. I also looked for signs of foul play such as a hole in the skull where a bullet might have passed, or a club that might have been used, broken limbs or even something buried with the bones such as a knife or club. But there was nothing.

I guessed the skeleton was very old but complete, although it would require an expert to determine the truth.

'Thanks, Ned. There's nothing more I can do here. It needs our experts to have a look next. I'll radio divisional headquarters from my bike so we can return to the house. I'll wait near my bike in case there are any radio messages.'

'You'll not need me anymore?'

'Not until the experts arrive, they might want a chat.'

'I'll be around, Mr Rhea.'

We returned to the house where I radioed divisional HQ with the full circumstances. I suggested they might care to summon the Scenes of Crime Department and also a forensic pathologist. Next I called Sergeant Blaketon at Ashfordly to tell him about the remains and he said he would drive immediately to Moorside Grange. And so a murder-style enquiry was set in motion. In such cases, we took no chances, treating all such mysterious deaths as suspected murder until the contrary was proved. In my own mind, this had all the appearances of a body having been buried on the moor many centuries ago, although the circumstances of the person's death and reason for his remote grave might only be guessed.

Within an hour teams of experts began to arrive and all were treated to Jenny's cups of tea and a selection of cakes. A forensic scientist with expertise in medieval burials arrived from Durham University and a pathologist with similar experience came from Middlesbrough. A local archaeologist had also been summoned and he turned up after all the others; among it all were several police officers including Sergeant Blaketon and myself. There was a lot of grave-side discussion that did not involve either me or Sergeant Blaketon; lots of official photographs were taken and samples removed from the grave itself and from the skeleton.

It took a long time—I had arrived on the scene around 2.30 p.m. and at six in the evening, everyone was still there. Jenny's cakes were being consumed at an alarming rate, albeit at some distance from the scene of operations as we did not want the scene contaminated with modern crumbs. When the time came to remove the remains, I summoned Alf Ventress in Ashfordly Police Station who said he would drive out with the shell. The shell was a large anonymous brown plastic coffin that fitted discreetly into the rear of a police van, and was used to remove bodies from crime scenes, fatal accidents or instances of sudden death. Ambulances were not used to carry dead bodies—they were for living people.

The remains were taken to a forensic pathology laboratory at Durham University because it specialized in medieval remains and artefacts—it seemed some tiny remnants of clothing, shoes and a belt had been found and it was thought they could be dated and perhaps identified as a particular item of wear. We were told that the detailed scientific investigation could take a few weeks to complete, but a provisional decision could be made about the age of the bones, which would be conveyed to us as soon as possible, probably within a week. Even while at the scene, however, the experts expressed their opinion that this was a very ancient skeleton with no signs of injury or assault upon the bones. The general consensus was that we would not be investigating a crime of murder, either ancient or modern.

Ned was given permission to fill in the grave if he wished but he said he would build his bield on another site. He'd fill in the grave with stones and earth from the surrounding moorland in case someone or something fell into the open grave and injured themselves. There would be nothing left to indicate this had once been a grave but, as Ned said, 'There was nowt to say so anyway, down all these years.'

There was some press interest in the story but when the initial results came through by telephone, we were told that the tiny pieces of clothing could be dated to around the fourteenth century. The same applied to the portions of leather from the shoes and belt, while the bones were also thought to date from that period. There were more detailed examinations yet to be completed. The coroner had been informed when the body was found but in the circumstances, he ordered that no inquest was necessary and issued a burial certificate.

A full written report, compiled by the experts, would follow within a week or two, but meanwhile the bones would be buried with a full requiem mass in the Roman Catholic graveyard at Maddleskirk Abbey, that being the country's undisputed 'old' religion during the period, although not then using the qualifying term 'Roman'. I made a point of attending as the only mourner.

The full written report was published a month later and its very detailed contents confirmed the date as the fourteenth century. The deceased had been a male aged about twenty-five at the time of his death and no injuries had been found to the bones, neither was there evidence of rheumatism or other bone diseases. Due to a lack of bodily tissues, it was not possible to ascertain whether the deceased had suffered from any disease or heart condition that might have contributed to his lonely death, but he had not died by the violent act of another. In other words, the cause of death was unknown and, furthermore, the identity of the young man could not be ascertained.

One of the puzzles was how his remains had come to be covered with a large flat stone and several smaller ones. That suggested that in the past there had been some kind of human involvement in the concealment of the remains.

Ned confirmed that he'd never had any inkling of the presence of a corpse on that moor and he had not covered, buried or reburied the remains; neither, to his knowledge, had any of his ancestors. We could only guess at the reason—according to the experts, the young man had died on the moor, probably alone, and he might have been trying to find shelter or rest in the hollow where he was found. If he had died there, someone many years ago might have come across the remains and, being unable to transport them to a formal grave, had covered them with those stones in that natural hollow. That was nothing but a guess although it seemed feasible.

But one other curious factor was contained in the report. I had received a copy of it with the suggestion that I allow Ned and Jenny Lofthouse to study it too. Apparently the man's leather belt had contained a small pouch that had survived because it had been protected by stones and had remained free from contamination all those years. Inside were the remains of some leaves and the experts had identified them as being from herbs—they named them as parsley, sage, rosemary and thyme. From my researches into the song about Scarborough Fair, I knew the writer of the famous folk verses spoke of seeking his loved one at the fair and that parsley, sage, rosemary and thyme were featured in all his verses.

So had this young man been heading for Scarborough Fair to seek his beloved girlfriend when death had overtaken him? He was only a few miles away from the path that led to Scarborough, the one where the Henry VII coins had been found. There was no money with his remains so was he the man who had lost all those coins? Or could he really have been the man whose absent love featured in that famous song? Perhaps he had asked a passer-by to look out for his girl to deliver the messages that are contained in the ten verses, or could he actually be the man who had written the words that begin with:

Are you going to Scarborough Fair?
Parsley, sage, rosemary and thyme,
Remember me to one who lives there
For she once was a true love of mine.

5. FAIR GAME

Once every two years Lord Ashfordly held a game fair in
the spacious grounds of Ashfordly Hall. It was a splendid
occasion that lasted for three days and was always on the
Tuesday, Wednesday and Thursday of the second week of
June. June was selected because it was widely reputed to be
a warm, dry month with lots of sunshine and long hours of
daylight, ideal for an open-air event. The truth was it could
often be cold, wet, windy and heavy with mist. Flaming June
is something of a legend!

However, whatever the weather the game fair was
enthusiastically supported by members of the landed gen-
try and lesser estate owners who lived in the North Riding
of Yorkshire. It attracted some who lived further afield, as
well as those who thought they were of equal status to the
county's estate owners. These were people who lived in big
houses and rode to hounds, funding their lifestyle by what
is euphemistically called new money, but their accents and
general demeanour usually revealed the truth. The game fair
was also patronized by large numbers of what are described
as ordinary people—that means working folk, like you and
me. They came along, as they put it, 'to see how the other
half lives'. But the game fair offered a great deal of interest

to all sections of rural society. From my point of view, it was fascinating to observe the clear distinctions in wealth, accent, styles of dress and the way people dealt with their alcoholic drinks or mud on their boots.

In rural Britain, the word 'game' is far-reaching and does not restrict itself to someone willing to take a risk such as being 'game for a laugh', nor does it apply only to sports such as football or cricket. It can apply equally to games played at home or in the pub such as snakes-and-ladders, dominoes, cribbage, card games, shove ha'-penny or darts. In rural England, the word has a further important meaning: it refers to a particular group of animals, fish and birds that are protected by the poaching laws but which are nonetheless pursued legally in the name of sport. Indeed, the anti-poaching laws are known as game laws and they seek to protect several species of wild creatures collectively known as game. Most country people are aware that poachers seek to make a good living by trespassing to take game of various kinds unlawfully. Such characters could not be charged with theft because the game is invariably wild and thus belongs to no one. As a consequence, parliament produced the offence of trespassing on land in the pursuit of game. In that way, their lordships, who made the laws, managed to protect the game that lived, fed and bred upon their estates.

The term 'game' includes pheasants, snipe, woodcock, red grouse, black grouse and their eggs, deer, rabbits and hares, salmon, trout, eels and migratory fish and their roe. It does not include foxes, otters or badgers, and there are separate laws to protect rarer wild creatures and even flowers and plants. Big game hunting, of course, is quite different—it is foreign for a start, and its game are very large and dangerous creatures.

With dodgy characters like Claude Jeremiah Greengrass living upon my beat, I did my best to be *au fait* with the poaching laws. But I needed to learn more than the law—I had to become knowledgeable about the means by which he and his kind managed to operate despite those laws while under the scrutiny of gamekeepers, estate owners and police officers. Poachers were full of tricks so it was a never-ending battle of wits.

In very general terms, a poacher would use stealth under the cover of darkness aided with such tools as nets, gaffs and bright lanterns. One trick, so we were led to believe, was to soak currants or raisins in whisky and then spread them on the ground for the pheasants to eat. Having eaten their fill, the birds would then fly up to their roosts but would be too drunk to fly off when the poachers arrived. There were even tales of them toppling off their perches and going to sleep on the ground in a drunken stupor to provide easy picking for poachers. There were fearsome stories of armed poachers using explosives to stun salmon and trout in the rivers while others used decoys to attract wild fowl within range of their special guns.

There is no doubt some derived a useful income from their poaching skills, often as a spare-time occupation that provided a tax free supplement to their day job. Many drove out from towns and cities, sometimes in gangs and often armed with clubs or other weapons, to raid country estates, large and small, for prizes of bags of pheasants, hares or rabbits. In large-scale poaching attacks, gamekeepers and even police officers could be attacked and beaten. That sort of poaching was therefore far more serious than a local rogue like Greengrass picking up the occasional rabbit or pheasant for the family supper.

But life in the great British countryside comprises far more than the antics of poachers and by attending game fairs it is possible to gain some insight into country life, however shallow that initial insight might be. Because these events concentrate upon the rural way of living in all its variety, it follows they are essentially linked to a wealth of countryside interests, sports, occupations, crafts and other skills. Game fairs offer little of real interest to a townsperson or a casual tourist, although some do turn up out of sheer curiosity. Game fairs are a specialized form of entertainment, not in the remotest sense being in the same league as funfairs, street fairs, mop fairs, fossil fairs, horse fairs, goose fairs or village fairs. In very general terms, they cater largely for people who live and work in the countryside and support every kind of hunting, or earn a living from it. That includes fox hunting, falconry, angling, whether by fly or live bait, the shooting of game birds such as partridges, pheasants or grouse, or even the taking of animals like rabbits and hares. It is not merely the chase that is involved—rural craftspeople will make all the specialized equipment necessary to pursue a particular sport such as nets, traps for vermin, fishing rods and much more, including shotguns and rifles.

All such products will be on sale or display at a game fair. There will be demonstrations of the skills used to create objects of many kinds—saddles and harness, shepherd's crooks and walking sticks, cartridge belts and gun bags, fence posts and gates, ropes and pond-liners. Clothing that is sufficiently well made to tolerate battles with briars and hawthorn hedges, as well as to keep the wearer warm and dry in all weathers is always a crowd-puller, not to mention accessories like wellington boots, gaiters, waterproof hats and bite-proof gloves. On show will be modern examples of ride-on grass cutters, tipping carts, corn bins, sheep clippers, bullock mangers, horse boxes, feeding troughs and gardening accessories of every kind. Because country-house gardens tend to be rather like municipal parks in size and content, the necessary tools will range from simple spades and rakes to complicated greenhouse watering systems, via combine harvesters and helicopters used for spraying chemicals. It is even possible to buy cream separators, pet food, rugs and wine racks, archery sets, canoes, tennis courts, swimming pools, croquet sets, nest boxes, hen-houses, greenhouses and saunas. The manufacturers all have stalls or displays where the equipment can be inspected or tested, and orders placed.

As well as commercial aspects of a game fair, there are competitions that include cross-country races, fly casting, clay-pigeon shooting, sheep-dog trials, hound trails, show jumping or point-to-point races as well as trotting contests. Magnificent shire horses and giant bulls may be decorated with brasses and garlands, then judged for the quality of their appearance; there are sheep shearing and best clip-rug contests along with 'Guess the weight of the pig' competitions.

One may also discover shows of the finest foods such as home-made cheese, jam, marmalade, chutney, fruit cakes and pork pies. Wines from the finest vines are sold while home-made products using natural ingredients like cowslips or plums are very popular. There are flower displays galore along with plants that can be used as hedgerows to provide privacy for both people and wild birds. All kinds of artwork by children and adults inevitably find a place at the game fair. In other words there is something rustic for everyone. On one occasion I was intrigued by a man walking home with a chimney-sweeping brush and another carrying a boot scraper, each no doubt being considered a prize trophy.

One would have thought the police were not necessary at such prestigious events, but on the first occasion I was the incumbent of Aidensfield during a game fair, Lord Ashfordly expressed a wish, through the chief constable, that a uniformed police presence would be welcome. He went to considerable lengths to say no trouble or crime was anticipated, but felt a police presence would add a touch of confidence and reassurance to the entire proceedings. That resulted in a memo from the chief constable to Sergeant Blaketon to suggest he set up a meeting with Lord Ashfordly to discuss the police arrangements for traffic control.

A suggestion of that kind was tantamount to an order.

'After all,' mused Lord Ashfordly to Sergeant Blaketon during one of those pre-game fair meetings in his oak-panelled study at which I was present, 'country folk, especially those who attend our game fairs are noted for their breeding, intelligence and good behaviour. I do not anticipate any kind of law-breaking or disturbance, so maybe your men can come along and take control of the car-parking?'

'There will be an officer patrolling in town, sir, and another at the entrance to your grounds, their duty being to control traffic away from the site. We shall staff the necessary points two hours before the fair begins and two hours afterwards to ensure a smooth flow of traffic both in and out of your grounds. I am confident that will be sufficient police coverage on the day.'

'I was thinking of a constable being stationed inside the ground, Sergeant,' said Lord Ashfordly very pointedly. 'It is the car-parking that concerns me, not the drivers' mode of arrival and departure.'

'We need constables on duty outside the grounds, my lord. The smooth regulation of traffic is vital to the town; we do not want any congestion that will interfere with the town's daily routine, or disrupt the workforce and townspeople. And we have to bear in mind the possibility of rapid access being required by the emergency services.'

'Yes, Sergeant, I fully understand that and I am sure you and your officers will provide the very best of service both to the town and its people. But once inside our grounds, drivers will need expert guidance into the parking area and then out again via our one-way system. And don't forget the exhibitors' transport; there will be a large number of lorries, vans and caravans coming and going at all times. As I made clear to the chief constable, I want officers on duty inside the grounds to make sure no vehicle is trapped and that everyone can get in and out when required, with no undue delays or hold-ups. And, of course, there is the question of security of all vehicles once their drivers and passengers have left—I do not want thieves of any kind operating on my land, especially during my game fair.'

'With all respect, my lord, car-parking *inside* the grounds is not the concern of the police. That is private premises—the responsibility rests with the organizers. It is they who should provide trained attendants who will take responsibility for car-parking.'

'But damn it all, man, there are police on duty at York Races on race days, and they are inside the course . . .'

'They are hired, my lord; the race company pays for them to be there. It's the same when police officers are on duty during the making of films or television programmes in public places. The officers perform such duties in their spare time, or during their rest days; they are paid overtime for the work and the cost is reimbursed to the police authority by the filmmakers, racecourse authorities or whatever. They are hired for such events, and the cost is not cheap.'

'I don't believe I'm hearing this, Blaketon! This is not what I expected. Over the years, my family and I have always had police officers in the grounds to supervise car-parking during the game fair. It is a major social and business event, Sergeant, you cannot ignore that. It's a showpiece for the district. It must be skilfully organized down to the very last detail.'

'My understanding of the situation, my lord, is that the chief constable agreed to your request for officers to undertake traffic duty during the course of the fair, but they will have to be outside your grounds at strategic locations. Unless, of course, you are willing to hire police officers to park the cars in the manner I have just described. To be honest with you, it would be cheaper to hire trained civilian car-park attendants and dress them in highly visible outfits. That is now happening at racecourses throughout Britain.'

'I have never in my entire life paid for the services of a constable to park cars, Sergeant.'

'Things are changing, my lord—'

'Changing? For the worse, they are! I might add I am renowned for my entertaining at the hall. Dinners, banquets, parties, wedding celebrations, civic functions, conferences— you name it and I've hosted it in style. And every occasion has been served by a uniformed police officer in charge of parking, without me paying any fees for his services.'

'That was in the past, my lord.'

'But one expects that level of service to be maintained in a civilized society, Sergeant. The country is going to the dogs.'

'That may be your opinion, my lord, but as I said, times are changing. New procedures are in place. We cannot provide full police cover for private events on private premises, so a request of this kind—car-parking at a private function— must now be treated as an essentially private matter.'

'I don't know what to say, Blaketon, you astound me.'

'Think of it like this, my lord. Suppose a constable on duty inside your grounds, parking cars and exhibitors' vehicles at one of your events, was run down and severely injured. Would you pay him any compensation, or provide a pension for him if he was compelled to retire on grounds of ill-health?'

'Now you are being absurd, Blaketon. One expects better of an experienced officer such as yourself The police run their own show, I run mine. Of course I would expect the force to pay for the outcome of any such injury; it would not be my responsibility.'

'Yes, it would be your responsibility, my lord. The force will compensate an officer who is injured during the performance of his duty, but parking cars at a private function is not part of his duty. That is a very important legal distinction. It is not his duty to park cars on private premises.'

'But we are abandoning years of service to the public, Blaketon. My God, this is awful, I don't know what the world is coming to.'

As I was a bystander during this verbal battle of wills, I could sense Sergeant Blaketon had scored a win as he continued, 'However, my lord, despite what I have just told you, I can arrange for a uniformed constable to parade through your grounds from time to time during the game fair, to be alert for law-breaking—pick-pockets, thieving and so forth. That comes within the scope of police duty, my lord—it is under the umbrella of prevention and detection of crime.'

'You know me well enough to be sure I shall always encourage the police to do their duty, Sergeant. Both you and I, as former military men, know the importance of that.'

'Thank you, my lord. I must say the decision is not mine.'

'I do understand that, Blaketon, but I must say I am extremely angry and disappointed by this unwelcome development. I shall have further words with the chief constable who, as you well know, is a friend of mine. I am sure he can overrule silly decisions that are made in the Home Office, the Council Chamber or wherever.'

'Would you care to ring him now, my lord? While I am present? I think you will find that these changes are beyond the scope of a chief constable's local decision-making. They are now a matter of national policy; we were informed through a Home Office circular.'

'It's all the government's fault, Blaketon. So, if I can't have a police presence to help me park those vehicles, what can you offer?'

'As I said, my lord, I can arrange for an officer to do a regular patrol through your grounds for the duration of the fair, preventing crime and so forth. And there will be officers on traffic duty outside the grounds.'

'So for the actual parking of the visitors' cars, and to ensure a free flow at all times for all vehicles, I must recruit my own attendants?'

'Yes, and it would be much cheaper than hiring police officers, my lord, and just as effective.'

'So your officers would patrol the car park too? Keep an eye open for thieves and vandals, that sort of thing?'

'They would be instructed to do so as part of their duty, provided you do not object to their presence! And I am sure that if there is any problem on the car-parking area, my officers will deal with it.'

'Then I consider that a good compromise, Blaketon. I do find this all very confusing, but I shall go along with your sensible recommendations. Maybe you know a good recruiting agency for car-parking attendants?'

'All I can suggest, my lord, is that your secretary contact the organizers of the classic car rally held last month at Elsinby Manor, the Cunninghams' place. They used professional car-parking attendants and there were no problems.'

'Leave this with me, Blaketon. If I encounter further difficulties, I shall be in touch. But I look forward to seeing your officers patrolling my grounds during the three-day fair, all in the line of their duty, of course.'

'Yes, my lord.'

We left and Sergeant Blaketon drove me back to Ashfordly Police Station where I had parked my motor bike. Before we parted, he said, 'Well, Rhea, you would learn a good deal from that meeting. Times are changing and quite honestly we have better things and more important things to do than parking cars at private events. We are no longer at the beck and call of people like Lord Ashfordly; the days of touching our forelocks have gone. But we still have our duty to perform and a uniformed police presence never goes amiss at any such gathering. We must be invited, however, because, as I made clear to Lord Ashfordly, his grounds are private property. The general public cannot walk in—it is a section of the public who will be attending, ostensibly at his lordship's invitation, even if they do have to pay. I am happy we have been invited to the game fair and I think it an interesting means of becoming *au fait* with rural matters. As a matter of fact, most of Ashfordly estate lies upon your beat so it is within your area of responsibility. Reserve the dates in your diary and I shall complete the necessary duty sheets in due course.'

A few weeks later I found myself patrolling the game fair on all three days, starting my duties at 10 a.m. and continuing until 6 p.m., a straight eight-hour shift.

The exhibitors and trade stands had arrived earlier and I noted the presence of police officers at the key traffic points in town; there was also a special entrance for those arriving on foot and I was pleased to see that the car-parking arrangements were well in hand. Large clear signs indicated the way into the car-parking areas for both visitors and exhibitors, and I noted the presence of attendants who were wearing bright yellow jackets emblazoned on the back with CAR-PARKING. From what I could see, they appeared to be very efficient because cars were being guided into a herringbone style of parking which resulted in the minimum of delay both on arrival and departure. The area comprised three large flat fields close to the entrance, all within easy walking distance of the exhibits and competitions. The marquees, tents, stalls, display caravans and temporarily located wooden exhibition cabins covered a huge level area below Ashfordly Hall while the parade ring was immediately in front of the big house with tiered viewing platforms and ringside seats.

It was a warm and sunny day, perhaps with rather more cloud than some would have liked, but it was dry with a strong southerly breeze. Visitors were arriving in their hundreds and a loud hailer was directing them to various sites and exhibitions while highlighting places such as the first aid tent, lost property office, lost children's playground, picnic sites, ice-cream kiosks, toilets and refreshment marquee. The announcer also heralded events in the ring—currently there was a display of driving a coach and four, with two magnificent teams each of four Cleveland Bays. One was hauling a beautifully preserved Wellington stagecoach that used to run on the Great North Road, the other was a similarly preserved Royal Mail coach.

Things seemed to be going well which meant I could relax and enjoy the fun of the fair. I began my steady patrol of all corners of the fair, marvelling at some of the exhibits shown by professional craftspeople or admiring the art of anglers as they cast flies at distant targets. The skills of shepherds herding small flocks of sheep into confined spaces merely by whistling commands to their dogs was always fascinating while the falconry demonstrations with goshawks and Harris hawks were of constant interest. And then a middle-aged man with a bald head and little round spectacles materialized from the crowds and came up to me.

'Officer, I think you should be aware of some animal cruelty over there.' He pointed towards a clutch of cabins and tents I had not yet visited.

'Where exactly?'

'It's along that route they call Heather Lane. There's a lot of cabins and tents and small exhibitions. It's a big cabin, number 49.'

'Right, so what kind of cruelty are you suggesting?'

'I think there is a gathering of men doing something nasty to ferrets,' he said. 'There's a sign above the entrance saying 'Ferrets' but this is no exhibition, Officer, it's a shouting match of some kind. It sounds dreadful, as if they are torturing the creatures, or making them fight. It sounds rather like a cock fight and that's illegal, as you know.'

'Have you been in to see what's going on?'

'No, I thought it wiser to stay away.'

'Maybe they're listening to a horse race on the radio at full volume?'

'I doubt it, Officer. From the noise they were making I'd say it's ferret baiting or something similar. And on top of all that, surely the animals will be distressed by a noisy crowd surrounding them?'

'Will you come and show me? I might need you as a witness.'

'Oh, no, even though I abhor cruelty to animals, I don't want to get involved. I was just passing . . .' And as he walked away, he said, 'I shall come back, Constable, I really do want you to halt this dreadful behaviour.'

'But I might need you as a witness . . .' I called after him, also asking for his name and address, but he ignored me and rapidly disappeared into the crowd. I could imagine him writing anonymous letters to the press about things that annoyed him, but without a witness, it would be difficult for me to proceed with a prosecution if indeed there was any law-breaking. I did not have the power to arrest the fellow and compel him to provide the necessary evidence, but decided I ought to follow up his complaint. If there was any cruelty to ferrets, then I could be the prosecution witness who was 'acting on information received' as my report would claim.

As I approached No. 49, Heather Lane from Moorland Walk, I noticed the banner on the cabin next door. It was the

RSPCA—they had a display inside with leaflets to take away and forms to complete if anyone wished to join or merely give a donation. I reasoned that if there were any cruelty, surely they would know. I decided to call in before taking any further action.

'Good morning.' There was a uniformed man at the counter inside. 'Can I help you, Constable? I am Inspector Blenkin of the RSPCA.'

'Nice to meet you.' We shook hands. 'It's just a quick query. I've just had an anonymous complaint that there is cruelty to animals next door, in the ferret display.'

'No, I've had a look; there's a lot of noise but no problem, Constable, I can assure you of that. Some people get upset by all the shouting and cheering, but the ferrets are fine. Pop into the ferret house and have a look for yourself; they're a friendly crowd. Who was the complainant?'

'I've no idea. He wouldn't give me his name and refused to act as a witness.'

'Then you're entitled to ignore him, but to put your mind at rest, go and have a look and then come and tell me what you think.'

'Thanks, I'll do that,' and I left.

As I approached the ferret house, I thought the idea of numbering the huts and naming the avenues was a good one. It simplified the problem of finding one's way around the extensive site by using the map provided with each entry ticket. As I grew closer, there was some unusually excited activity inside No. 49. It was certainly generating far more interest than most of the other displays. It was a substantial wooden cabin with the front facing wall opening to provide a view into the interior. There was a door to the right of that opening but both the door and the viewing area were full of men all shouting and cheering. When I drew nearer, I could see the interior was also full of men in a highly excited mood.

I had no idea what could be happening inside, but across the front was the legend *FERRETS* in large white lettering. Perhaps this place contained cages of different types of ferret?

Perhaps there might be a polecat, or a polecat-ferret, or even a mink or two, or one of those beautiful pine martens that inhabit our northern forests? Those animals, including otters, stoats and weasels, are related to the domestic ferret, and until today I had never realized ferrets were so popular. As I headed for the open door, the shouting and cheering subsided as it turned into normal chatter—I was reminded of a crowd watching a horse race, cheering the winner home but lapsing into near silence once the result was known. When the men crowded in the doorway realized I was fast approaching, they eased away so that I could enter.

'Come for a flutter, have you, Constable?' asked one. 'You should put it on number 13, it comes up time and time again.'

'A flutter?' I tried to be jocular with them. 'I can't place bets, I'm in uniform and on duty. Besides, what is there to place a bet on?'

'Ferdinand,' the man said. 'He's running next. Loves number 13, he does. Unlucky for some, but not him.'

It was then, as I moved deeper inside the cabin that I realized I had never seen bookmakers attending a game fair. It seems they did not frequent this type of event so there was no one to open books and run bets on competitions like four-in-hand coach-driving, sheep-dog trials, fly casting, hound trails, clay-pigeon shooting and so forth. It was probably not worth their while for such specialized and limited punters. When I reached the interior, it was also crowded with men looking into a type of arena in the centre of the room. My heart sank as a familiar voice grumbled, 'Oh, it's not you, Constable Rhea, is it?'

'Claude Jeremiah Greengrass! I should have known you'd be somewhere here today, but what on earth is going on? And why all the shouting and noise?'

Around the interior walls were several cages each containing a ferret and I guessed this was some kind of ferret show. Each of the cages bore a separate number. The arena in the centre of the room comprised a square enclosure surrounded by a wooden wall about a yard (1 m) high. Each of the four lengths of the wall was about four yards long (4 m or so) and the floor was covered with a thin layer of straw. There was a gate in one of the walls. The whole thing reminded me of the sort of pen a child would use in which to keep pet rabbits or hens. However, it differed from a rabbit pen because in the centre, instead of a hutch or hen-house there was a large plump beer barrel that was about three feet high (1 m) and a couple of feet or so (60 cm) wide at its broadest point. Around the base of the barrel was a series of round holes about two inches apart and each being about four inches (10cm) in diameter. There were twenty holes each with a white number painted above it in sequence of 1 to 20. And running around the interior of the wall was a ferret. So it was some kind of ferret event, I reasoned.

'Come for a flutter have you, Constable Rhea?' asked Greengrass. 'Only a quid a go.'

'A flutter, Claude? I don't know what you are talking about, but I've had a complaint about cruelty to ferrets.'

'Cruelty to ferrets? What are *you* talking about?'

'A man outside; he told me there was cruelty to ferrets going on in here . . .'

'And you believed him?' Claude sounded incredulous at such a thought. 'That man obviously knows nowt about ferrets or country sports and neither do you by the sound of things. That surprises me, seeing how you're the bobby of Aidensfield.' And the crowd of men cheered at that remark.

'I told him I would investigate his complaint,' was my attempt at a suitable answer. I looked around the cages and all the ferrets seemed content and without injury, not that I could really be certain from where I was standing. The one running around inside the arena seemed quite happy and free and I noticed an empty cage, doubtless it's home for the duration of the fair.

'Well, there you are, Constable, take a look and ask the ferrets if you're not happy. They'll tell you they are the best-kept ferrets in England, well fed and watered with plenty of food and comfortable homes.'

'Best-kept ferrets this side of the Grand Canyon,' said one man.

'Best anywhere in the world,' put in another.

Again, this produced a few chortles from the assembled spectators and I could see that Claude was enjoying his moment of fun with the constabulary. But constabulary duty had to be done and I was duty bound to ask, 'So what is going on, Claude?'

'Well, consider this as part of your rural education, Constable Rhea, but this is ferret roulette.'

'Ferret roulette? So how does that work?'

'Look, you're holding up the proceedings by all your daft questions, so I think the best thing is for me to show you a practical demonstration. So just stand there and watch.'

He went into the arena and picked up the ferret, returning it to the empty cage (No. 7). There were twenty cages around the walls each containing a single animal. That meant twenty ferrets. All were now full. So far, so good.

'Right,' said Greengrass to me, with the assembled men now quiet and watchful. 'We select one of those ferrets by picking a ball out of a bag. Seeing you are our guest, you can do it,' and from his pocket he produced a green cloth bag, shook it and invited me to dip into it and lift out a small ball. I did so and it bore the number 9.

'Right,' he said. 'That means ferret number nine runs in our next competition. Now it's time to place your bets, lads.'

From a desk beside the ferret cages, Claude produced four metal money boxes of the kind that most people used for their household expenditure. Each was about a foot long (30cm) with five coin slots in the lid at intervals; people would use these to set aside cash for things like insurance, electricity, gas, petrol, newspaper bills, the milkman or church collections. In this case, each of the wide slots was marked by a number, one of the boxes numbering 1-5, another 6-10, another 11-15 and the final one showing numbers 16-20.

'Right, lads,' shouted Claude. 'Here we go. The constable has selected ferret nine, that's Clarence. Get your bets on.'

He passed the tins among the men and the assembled multitude dropped or pushed their bets into their chosen slots of the boxes. I noticed that each punter also pushed into the slot what appeared to be a coloured cloakroom ticket, folded in half. I was to learn later that they had already written their names on the backs of those tickets. It cost a pound to bet on each number, most being paid by pound notes being thrust through the holes—they were wide enough to accommodate notes—although some men used coins or a mixture of coins and notes. Eventually, the heavy boxes of cash were returned to Claude. That exercise took at least quarter of an hour.

'Fancy a go, Constable?'

'Why not?' I responded. 'I can claim I am researching the complaint about cruelty. So, what am I betting on?'

'You're betting on which hole at the bottom of the barrel is used by the ferret when he comes out. The numbers on the lids of these cash boxes correspond to the numbers above the holes around the bottom of the barrel.'

He paused to allow me to study the import of what he was saying.

'We put the ferret in the barrel, you see, placing him inside through the lid at the top—it lifts off—and there's a ferret ladder running the full length inside down to the bottom.' He removed the top of the barrel to show me the internal area—it was empty save for the small ladder. It was the type one would find at a hen-house entrance but a little longer albeit with ridges to provide a foot-hold.

The ferret would have no trouble coping with it.

'We place him at the top of that ladder so he doesn't fall down—no cruelty, you see, Constable. This is not as bad as going down a rabbit hole! And that's not considered cruel to ferrets, it's quite natural for them.'

'I'm with you so far.'

'Right, now you can see that all those holes around the bottom of the barrel are numbered so we are betting on which one he comes out of. Just like roulette.'

'So when a punter places his bet, he adds his name as well?'

'Aye, on a cloakroom ticket, they write them in advance. I supply the tickets. One of those small tickets fits into the slot of the tin. I give 'em all a book of cloakroom tickets when they arrive, it doesn't matter what colour they are or what numbers they have on, it's the names that matter.'

'You've thought it all out very well, Claude.'

'Aye, well, I'm not so daft as you think, Constable.'

'So we might find five pounds in one compartment inside the tin, only one in another, two or three in another and so on. Is there any limit on how many punters can bet on each ferret run?'

'Nope, no limit. The more the merrier. We've about forty chaps here today as you can see, so that could be a total of about forty quid in those boxes for every run. It's only a pound for each bet. Some might want to place more than one bet—no problem. It's all worth winning, eh? And you can see now, how we have a different ferret that is chosen at random for each run, so that the same hole isn't used on every occasion. We've no idea which hole each ferret favours. Dead honest we are, Constable.'

'So if I select hole thirteen, I need to put my pound in slot number thirteen on those boxes? I'm not betting on the ferret's number, but on the number above one of those holes at the bottom of the barrel?'

'Right, we look for the one the ferret comes out of.'

'I understand, Claude.'

'You're catching on fast.'

'So all I get back, if I win, is my pound—and if three of us bet on the same number, we all get our pound back—and everyone else loses their bets. I suppose you keep the rest! That's not much of a prize, Claude, am I right?'

'Not quite, Constable, that wouldn't make it worth-while, you've got that bit right. And there's no way these chaps would let me keep such a lot for my expenses. But you're right. Those who don't bet on the right number lose their stakes, that's true enough, but the winner—or win-ners—get a share of all the stakes.'

'Ah! So that does make it worthwhile? For them?'

'Aye, it does. So you see, if only one chap picks the right hole that the ferret comes out of, then he wins the lot. A return of up to forty quid or thereabouts for a one pound stake isn't bad.'

'It sounds OK to me.' But I now decided to have a little fun with the old rogue, a modest retaliation after his earlier jokes at my expense.

'Aye,' nodded Claude, his old eyes blinking at me. 'It's better than horse racing.'

'So what do you get out of this? It must cost quite a lot to set up a place of this kind, renting the space and so on.'

'I keep ten per cent of the income on each game.' He blinked.

'The income, not the profit?' I put to him.

'Well, sometimes there might not be a profit, but I have to run the show, pay for this place, get the cloakroom tickets and whatever. It costs me a lot of my time and expertise; I need to compensate myself for all that.'

'It's all very interesting, Claude, and I am happy that there is no cruelty to the ferrets. After all as you say, it's not as bad as being pushed down a dark rabbit hole to flush out prey, is it? And I can tell you, I did have a chat with the RSPCA man next door, he gave you the all-clear.'

'So your investigation is complete? I'm innocent; there's no suffering ferrets as I said, so, can I get on with my work?'

'Just another query, Claude.' I tried to adopt my most serious and official expression. 'Have you got a bookmaker's permit?'

'A bookmaker's permit? I'm not a bookie, Constable!'

'You are using premises where persons resort for betting transactions, and the premises concerned is not an approved racecourse, or a licensed dog racecourse, or a licensed betting office. That means you need a bookmaker's permit.'

Claude coughed, blinked and spluttered, then said, 'Hang on, Constable, you can't be serious . . .'

'Or we might classify your activities as a lottery, but to make that legal you might have to run it for charitable purposes, while on the other hand you could be guilty of unlawful gaming and, of course, if you are guilty of any of these offences, it is possible we might have to consider prosecuting Lord Ashfordly for allowing his premises to be used for one or other of those unlawful purposes . . .'

By this stage, the horrified expression on Claude's face caused me to break into a smile and he knew I was teasing him.

'You're having me on, Constable Rhea! You're making all this up, having a go at me . . .'

'All right, let's call a truce. I am not sure precisely what sort of gambling ferret roulette is, so I will put a pound on number thirteen,' and I handed him a note which he pushed into the necessary slot in one of the tins, following it by a cloakroom ticket bearing my name. The assembled men cheered as they realized I was not serious about Claude's illegalities—if indeed he was breaking the law. I thought his activity was a legal conundrum—certainly it was anything but straightforward.

When Claude was satisfied that all his customers had placed their bets, he lifted the ferret onto the ladder at the point nearest the top of the barrel and closed the lid. He then rushed through the gate into the compound to observe events and after a long delay, someone cheered. The tiny pink nose and eyes of the ferret were poking through hole No. 12 but he didn't emerge. The shouting caused him to retreat and everyone waited in silence as Clarence tried to decide which of the outlets to use. His nose appeared several times, each occasion raising cheers, but then he made up his mind. He bolted out of No. 13! I had won!

When Claude checked the contents of the compartments inside the tin, I was the only one who had bet on that hole and so I won everything, less Claude's expenses which, on this occasion, amounted to six pounds. It had been an interesting introduction to the sport of ferret roulette, but I decided not to mention it to Sergeant Blaketon. There was always the likelihood that he might decide to explore the situation further in an attempt to decide whether it was illegal betting, gaming or a lottery. But had I taken part in illegal betting?

'Gentlemen!' I shouted, as Claude paid me my winnings. 'I am classing my participation here as part of my investigation process, but because I am not sure about what happens next, I am not going to keep my winnings. I shall give them to the RSPCA next door, as a charity donation from us all. Does that suit you?'

Someone raised a cheer, then a man shouted, 'And you, Claude, you need to pay over your expenses on this one . . .'

He spluttered and muttered, but eventually gave me the six pounds. 'I'll hand it over now, and bring the receipt back to you. Thanks for the game, everyone.'

As I left, I heard him mutter, 'I'll get him for that', to which I responded, 'Fair game, Claude. Fair game.'

And so I donated my winnings and Claude's expenses to the RSPCA with the attendant expressing his genuine delight. I returned the receipt to the Ferret House just as Ferret No. 14 (Cuthbert) was about to start his run but I declined another opportunity to place a bet and continued my patrol of the game fair.

6. ALL'S FAIR IN LOVE AND WAR

One of the major lessons learned by rookie police officers is never to take sides in domestic disputes. Within the world of policing there are domestic disputes aplenty with most of them involving ordinary citizens, but occasionally similar fights break out among the ranks of serving police officers, or even vicars, doctors, or magistrates. Fortunately, I have never had to mediate in a battle between such protagonists, but if we did wade into domestic disputes of any kind it could be guaranteed that both parties would turn upon us. We would be accused of exacerbating the problem and would be blamed for causing the trouble in the first place. Such logic was difficult to understand.

Because 'domestics' were such a large part of our working lives, we were warned that there would be countless occasions when husbands and wives, boyfriends and girlfriends or even next-door neighbours, would be seen fighting and arguing in and around their own homes. Sometimes they would allow their anger to spill into the street and that's when the affair could concern the police because neighbours would ring up to sound the alarm bells.

Strictly speaking, the resolution of a 'domestic' was not within the scope of police duty—it was a matter for a solicitor,

116

a domestic court of law or the combatants themselves. The police did their best not to become involved, even if neighbours or holidaymakers were fighting about high hedges, blocking access to one's property, too much noise, disputing a parking space, squabbling over deck-chairs, getting angry about a careless word or forgotten anniversary, arguing about the non-settlement of a debt or loan, or simply fighting.

Despite a multitude of hidden problems, this was an interesting area of law even if it was regarded as part of police duty. What particularly intrigued young, idealistic police officers was that so many adults could find so many things to fight about. Frequently that anger became public and a splendid source of entertainment. Some disputes could be predicted—it was known, for example, that Mr and Mrs Barnstormer from Holly Gables would always fight on a Saturday night when they got home from the pub. The police and neighbours knew all about it, the cause invariably being that Mr Barnstormer could not keep his eyes—and sometimes his hands—off barmaids with low-cut dresses. Across the nation, there were probably millions of battles on a Saturday night, most of which did not impinge upon the population's permanent state of bliss and tranquillity.

Of course, in our part of rural Yorkshire, not every domestic dispute came to the notice of the police. Most were quietly dealt with by the families, or sometimes with aid and advice of discreet neighbours. We, the police, managed to keep our distance from the warring parties by stressing their dilemma was essentially a civil matter.

Our practice was to suggest they consult a solicitor. The same applied if an aggrieved person felt he or she had been badly treated by someone not paying their proper debts. It was very common for hard-working, self-employed business people to complete some work, or provide a service, only to discover they were never going to be paid. It is an undisputed fact that many customers persistently refuse to pay their bills even though the work is satisfactory. Failure to pay one's dues is a form of dishonesty, but it is not a criminal offence and therefore not a matter for the police. The police show interest if it involves fraud or false accounting, but such behaviour, minus proof of fraud, is categorized an 'unsatisfactory business transaction'.

Resolution might be achieved by a solicitor, or if not, through action in a civil court or in today's world, the Small Claims Court. Whether the police would ever get involved in such matters depends upon the precise circumstances and the available evidence.

If such battles, whether matrimonial, business-linked or neighbourly disputes, became violent and spilt into a public place, or if assaults or damage were part of the gladiatorial entertainment, it was likely the police would be summoned. The natural conclusion was that both parties were arrested. Quite often, that simple action resulted in a modicum of peace and sanity to prevent further trouble and a solemn promise to behave could often lead to their release. After all, the police did not want rowdy folks inhabiting their normally peaceful cells.

If we thought it necessary, however, the opposing parties would be taken before the magistrates' court on a charge of 'conduct likely to cause a breach of the peace' or for breaking some other law relating to public order. More often than not, the police would ask the magistrates to bind over the protagonists to be of good behaviour or to keep the peace. Such 'binding-over' orders might be subject to certain relevant conditions and they could remain effective for a number of years. Happily, binding-over orders were extremely effective and helped to maintain the peace for some time afterwards. If the offender committed the same offence again, or perhaps a similar one within the time limit, or if he or she breached any of the conditions imposed, then they could be punished with perhaps a fine, probation or even imprisonment.

It is not generally known that the law which created the power for magistrates to 'bind over' troublemakers in this magnificent and sensible manner was passed as long ago as 1360-61 during the reign of Edward III. During my time at Aidensfield that Act and its procedures were more than 600 years old and were still working very well indeed. If a real humdinger of a domestic battle did spill into the street or any public place, however, we would have to consider all the consequences and take any necessary action, particularly if assaults, injuries or damage were caused. Another point to consider was whether war would break out again, and again, and again.

If it were repeated within the happy family home, or even within its curtilage of their house, we would not wish to become involved even if the neighbours did complain. And, of course, we knew that some neighbours persistently complained about absolutely anything—in fact, we maintained lists of persistent complainers, most of whom were never satisfied whatever action was taken.

It was against this background that I and most of the constables of Ashfordly and Brantsford found ourselves inextricably involved with continuing reports of a never-ending battle between Brendan Patrick Conning and his wife Avis. No one was quite sure when or why the feud started, but it had been part of local life for many years. Gossip among police officers indicated the Connings had started fighting soon after their marriage although such a precise record was difficult to locate because they had never appeared in court. From what I learned, the rather doubtful history of the Connings' disputes had been spread by word of mouth and rumour, rather than solid evidence in the form of written records. As they were now in their mid-fifties, with children living away from home, it appeared that their hostilities were something akin to the Hundred Years War, or that Brendan was modelled upon Conn, a mythical Irish king nicknamed Hero of a Hundred Fights. Indeed there were some who reckoned Brendan Conning was a direct descendant of that famous king and that he was merely maintaining the family reputation.

As the original Conn was known for the hundred fights in which he had engaged during the second century, it followed that generations of Connings might now claim to have indulged in the region of 170,000 fights. However, our very localized lore indicated that most had occurred between Brendan and Avis when at home, and due to their persistent warfare, the couple had become rather notorious.

When I became the new constable of Aidensfield, I was soon to learn about the Connings, but it was some months before I made contact with them; most of their battles were attended by officers from either Ashfordly or Brantsford because the family home was not on my beat. The reason why the two towns' complement of police officers were involved was that the Connings' beautiful thatched home was situated almost exactly midway between them in the picturesque village of Graindale. It meant stories of their skirmishes spilt over into either of the nearby communities simply because the police from one of those towns would generally be called in to quell each new disturbance.

In many ways, it rested upon the local constabulary to decide how to deal with their quarrels. According to information passed on to me, their battles were frequently loud and violent, but the fact they were invariably at the family home meant that the normal laws relating to disturbance of the peace in tranquil places did not apply. In that way, the Connings had avoided any appearance in court.

A man's home (or a woman's for that matter) was his or her castle, a place of refuge where, in theory they could behave as they pleased. However, even though the Connings' outbursts were always within the home, the police could not ignore them if they terrified the neighbours and made the local dogs bark. Frequent verbal references to Brendan and Avis, even without the back-up of previous behaviour recorded in our files, had elevated many of their domestic rows into something that could legally be considered a breach of the peace, or a breakdown in public order if it had occurred in the street. But none did—that was the odd thing. Every rumpus was safely behind closed doors, or perhaps in the garden.

Graindale, the village that was their home, was located just off the main road halfway between Ashfordly and Brantsford, and it was distinguished by its collection of ancient thatched cottages that were in various states of repair. The one belonging to the Connings, a fine detached house set in its own grounds, was very well maintained and lay in a quiet corner of the village, so their indoor battles rarely reached any further than the ears of their immediate neighbours. In fact, one would have thought that even the noisiest party at the Connings' place would not inconvenience their neighbours due to the distance between the houses. However, we knew through local gossip that those indoor ding-dongs occurred because, so we had been told, it was often necessary for a painter and decorator to go in to repair the damage, or an electrician to replace broken lights. A glazier might be needed to fix broken windows or mirrors and a carpenter might be required to repair smashed chairs and other items of furniture. How many of those rumours were true and how many were little more than exaggeration was a matter of speculation. Nonetheless, the Connings' own chain of DIY shops provided many of the items necessary to effect speedy repairs because Brendan was too busy to carry out the work himself. He kept a lot of local tradesmen in business; they were very regular visitors to his home—or so I was told. As I studied past records, I thought there was very little evidence of their quarrelling—I had a feeling that their reputation appeared to be built on gossip and hearsay. I began to wonder why.

Both the Connings were interesting people; Brendan was a large bear of a man in his early fifties who stood at least six feet tall, with a mop of iron-grey hair on top of his round, florid face. He looked and spoke like a typically happy and contented Irishman, which he was. Powerfully built with broad shoulders and little sign of middle-aged spread, he had, in his youth, been a successful rugby player. He had also done well at sports like throwing the discus or javelin, and it was rumoured he had once won a Highland Games competition for tossing the caber. And the one sport he watched rather than participated was horse racing. He had a long and happy relationship with racehorses because he had a knack of selecting winners. He was also a highly successful businessman who had founded several busy DIY stores in neighbouring towns.

At the time, the notion of do-it-yourself was fairly new among townspeople, although country people had been doing it since Adam was a lad. Few self-respecting countrymen would ever consider getting a workman into the house or farm to fix something or to decorate the happy home—they did it all themselves and were skilled in most trades, from woodwork and stonework to electrical skills, to plumbing and fixing the car or tractor.

When living in Ashfordly as a young man prior to his marriage, Brendan had spotted a gap in the market and had established his first DIY store in Brantsford. Its rapid success meant another was opened in Ashfordly, then others in Galtreford and Eltering. He called them Tower Outlets, his reference to a tower probably coming from a veiled link to his own surname and the conning towers of submarines. Periscopes were housed in conning towers and they could look across the vastness of the normally unseen areas of ocean—just as Brendan's shops could cater for the interior beauty of the homes of masses of townspeople. His enterprise meant he made a lot of money in a very short time and his shops, and his luck with the horses, helped him to keep his own house in very good order with fine furnishings and modern décor.

Avis, a tall, smart woman with a slender figure and long blonde hair that belied her fifty years or so, wore a variety of eye-catching outfits both at home and at work. Before her marriage, she had trained as a secretary with a firm of accountants in Ashfordly. Her skills outside work were squash, tennis and badminton. She had met Brendan in a local gymnasium where he had been toning up for a charity run. At the time both were in their early twenties and both had noticed the other with more than a passing interest. From what I heard,

Brendan had abandoned his idea of running a half-marathon to marry Avis so they could spend happy times in the gym after a honeymoon skiing in Austria and mountaineering in the Alps.

Coincidentally, Brendan's booming business became desperately in need of clerical assistance from someone with both financial and clerical knowledge and so, in wooing Avis, he had found exactly the right person. She could share in the further development of his expanding empire. And what better than a man and wife working for their mutual benefit in a perpetual state of bliss and happy success?

What nobody had predicted was that Brendan and Avis could not apparently live together. No one knew why they could not tolerate one another at home, and at the same time it seemed they could not live without each other. That they loved one another was very obvious to all, and they were never frightened to say so in public or in the shop or anywhere else. They would regularly display their affection before their staff with lots of hugs and kisses.

According to PC Alf Ventress, the police had learned over the years that, during their busy workaday routine in running their business, there were no problems. The trouble was always centred upon their home.

'They're a lovely couple,' Alf told me once, when a complaint arose. 'Liked by everyone, successful in business, but we do get complaints about their behaviour at home, so we have to do something about it even if it's not really a police matter. We go along to calm things down.'

I did not have to deal with that particular complaint but I did ask, 'Alf, there's not a lot in our files about them. I've heard so much about their warring behaviour—'

'The complaints don't always come into this office,' he told me. 'The complainants might ring Brantsford police or one of the local rural beats. Different officers attend and sort things out without any paperwork; we don't take the couple to court so there are no files and we don't pool our knowledge. There's no need, it's only domestic problems. Word of their behaviour gets passed down by word of mouth as a rule. I am sure the neighbours know there is something amiss yet again when police cars turn up with flashing blue lights.'

I wondered how it was that if their house was located so far from their neighbours, they could complain. This concern was reinforced when I met the couple in one of their shops. Avis had her office in the Ashfordly store from where she maintained her records of all the other shops; Brendan had his office above the Brantsford store. Whenever they met, perhaps with their managers for a business meeting, they were models of patience, tolerance and mutual admiration. Each of the shops was supervised by a manager, and each shop had two other full-time members of staff, with part-timers being employed at busy periods like weekends.

Both Brendan and Avis paid separate but regular visits to all the stores and the couple were liked and respected by their employees and by their customers. There was absolutely no hint of any private turmoil.

Most of their domestic incidents had reputedly taken place before I was posted to Aidensfield and I admit I was sceptical about some of the recent reports. They seemed a bit vivid and far-fetched and I wondered if they had grown better with every telling—a common occurrence. Rumours do get better with repetition and, if the tales were to be believed, Brendan and Avis fought like a couple of gladiators—but always at home. Once or twice as more reports came in, always dealt with by another officer, I wondered how the police had become aware of them. Who had alerted them in the first place?

Without mentioning my concern to anyone, I began to question the reputation they had acquired. Although we kept no files about their behaviour, the daily Occurrence Books contained brief reports about call-outs to their home, but those records were far from comprehensive. Most of the entries recorded the fact that the police had visited the scene on request, but there was no index of such domestic call-outs. In some cases, the visit was concluded by giving 'suitable advice' to the warring couple and in other instances, the police had arrived only to find the house in darkness and at peace. In those cases, the entries were endorsed 'Attended scene, all quiet upon arrival'. At no time, had either of the couple appeared in court charged with a public order offence or to be bound over to keep the peace.

Clearly they were a complex couple and my first involvement with their *alter egos* occurred some time after my arrival at Aidensfield—as their home was not on my beat, I had not attended any complaint about their behaviour, even though I had heard such a lot about them. On that occasion I was performing a night shift in Ashfordly one Wednesday night and was looking after the enquiry office from 10 p.m. until 2 a.m. At midnight the phone rang and I answered, 'Police Office, Ashfordly. PC Rhea speaking.'

'You must come quickly, now; it's urgent; they're going to kill each other.' It was a woman's voice.

'Who is?'

'Brendan and Avis. You know their thatched cottage in Graindale? You've often been called out. The Connings. She's gone mad . . . it really is serious this time.'

'I'll be there in five minutes. Don't you go into the house as you could be in danger. And you are?'

'Their next-door neighbour, Julie Anson. Miss. I've never seen them as bad as this, Constable, it's frightening.'

'Right, I'm on my way.'

I rang Eltering Police Office to say I was leaving the Ashfordly station temporarily unattended while attending a domestic incident in Graindale.

'Don't get involved, Nick,' advised PC Rogers, the constable at the other end of the phone in Eltering. 'The Connings are regulars on our books; there's loads of complaints logged here and elsewhere, so don't get involved, don't take sides.'

'Don't worry, I'll cope.'

I had never been to the house and a few minutes later I eased into the drive with my blue light flashing. I left it flashing as I parked the car, booked off the air and climbed out. I thought the distinctive light might produce some kind of sobering effect; it might even calm the protagonists. In the lights of the car and of some other houses not far away, I could see the woman who had probably called me. She was a small person in her fifties with iron-grey hair, and was wearing a sweater and skirt. She approached me as I left my car at the garden gate.

'Oh, thank goodness you've come, Constable. I thought they were going to kill each other this time. You're new, aren't you?'

'Yes, I'm PC Rhea from Aidensfield. I was on duty in Ashfordly when you rang.'

'Thank you for coming so quickly. Look what they did, over there. On the lawn.' Her voice contained more than a tremor of excitement as she told me the story. She indicated a darkened window that had been smashed and told me she had witnessed a footstool come hurtling through the glass to land on the lawn and roll into the border. There was also a pair of ladies' black high-heeled shoes on the lawn. According to Miss Anson, they had been thrown through the hole in the glass to land on the lawn soon after the footstool. Much of the house was in darkness, but I could see a light inside, probably in the kitchen and all seemed to be calm indoors.

'It was me who rang the Ashfordly station. It's gone all quiet now,' she said. 'I'm sorry to drag you out, but I thought things were going to get out of hand. One of these days they'll do serious harm to one another . . .'

'So, which is your house?' I asked, wondering how she had heard any loud noises.

'Over there.' She pointed to a thatched cottage about a hundred yards away. 'Rose Bower it's called.'

'So do you know if they've been out tonight, to the pub? Would you know that?'

'I don't think so, Mr Rhea. I think they've had a quiet night in. Avis said they were going to do that tonight as it's their wedding anniversary. She told me this morning. She said that because they go out a lot for dinners in hotels and restaurants, she would like a night in. She told me she would cook a romantic meal for Brendan and herself, so they could be on their own with a bottle of champagne and some chocolates.'

'There's nothing I can do legally and, as you can see, it is all quiet now,' I had to remind Miss Anson. 'Domestic rows are of little concern to the police. Even damage to their own property can be beyond our scope. If they broke their own window I can't take action against them.'

'Not even if they cause injury?'

'If one attacks the other with fists, shovels, rolling pins or carving knives inside the marital home, we can't take action unless we get a formal complaint from the injured party. We can't compel a wife to give evidence against her husband, or vice versa . . . it's a very complicated area of law, but it usually means that if we do try to instigate proceedings against one or the other for a serious assault, neither will provide the evidence that we need for a hearing. So it's often a waste of our time.'

'But this sort of thing could lead to murder!'

'Which is why I am here to try and prevent them going that far. And yes, we can deal with very serious assaults and murders. As I said, it is a very complex area of law. So, let's see if I can get into the house and have a word with them. I'll warn them about their future conduct.'

'Shall I come? I am a neighbour and friend,' said Miss Anson. 'I do know them well. They're such nice people, really . . . I do care for them. I rang because I don't want to see them hurt . . .'

'I don't think you'd better come in, not just yet, not unless I need some help to soothe them or calm them down—I wouldn't want you to get hit by flying kitchenware or rolling pins. But if you wait outside . . .'

'Yes, I quite understand.'

It seemed very quiet inside the house as I approached the front door. I thought about picking up the shoes and footstool to take them back inside, but decided that action might remind them of whatever had caused this fracas. So I left them alone. Although part of the house was in darkness, there was a glow of lights through the opaque glass in the upper part of the door, and I thought I detected movement. Maybe I should have gone to the back door. Were they now in the kitchen? There was only one way to deal with this relatively minor matter so I switched off the rotating blue light of the car and then rang the front doorbell as Miss Anson watched from the shadows. I noticed that no other neighbours had ventured out, but their houses were some distance away.

As the bell shrilled, a light inside the entrance hall was switched on and so was another on the exterior above the door. I waited as the door was unlocked and then Avis appeared, as calm and as lovely as ever, with not a hair out of place and not a flush of guilt upon her beautiful face.

'Yes? Oh, it's the police. Do come in, Constable. It is late, but can I get you a cup of tea or coffee? Or perhaps something stronger?'

'No, nothing thank you. I am PC Rhea from Aidensfield and I am on duty—'

'Yes, I can see that. But do come in. We can't talk on the doorstep.'

She admitted me and closed the door after a quick glance at the scene outside. I was not sure if she had seen Miss Anson waiting and watching in the darkness. Avis halted inside the spacious hall and smiled. I noticed she had very dark blue eyes and a remarkably clear skin; she was a most attractive woman, but I sensed she had a powerful personality. She was immediately in control of the situation, behaving as if nothing untoward had occurred. My first impression was that nothing unusual had happened, it was all tidy, but I had not entered the room with the broken window.

'We have met, haven't we?' she asked.

'Yes, in the shop. I've often called in when I was off duty.'

'Of course, I recognize you now. So what can I do for you, Constable? It's usually officers from Ashfordly or Brantsford who come to see us.'

Before I could answer, a strong voice asked, 'Who is it, darling?' and Brendan appeared. He was also immaculate in a clean shirt and casual trousers. He was smiling warmly as he nursed a glass of what looked like brandy.

'Ah, the law!' he beamed amiably. 'But at this late hour? So how can we help, Constable? Can I get you a brandy? Whisky perhaps?'

'No thanks, I am on duty. I've received a complaint from one of your neighbours about the noise and what sounded like a serious attack—'

'Rubbish, Constable! Absolute rubbish. There has been no noise tonight; we've had the record-player on with some nice romantic music, but there has been no party. No singing or shouting. Avis and I have been quietly celebrating our wedding anniversary—our thirtieth would you believe, all on our own. No loud guests or noisy car doors.'

'That's the pearl wedding, Constable,' smiled Avis. 'And Brendan, my dear husband, gave me this lovely pearl necklace . . .' and she flashed it at me.

I thought their response was polite and charming and neither looked as if they had been involved in a fight, but they did not invite me any further into their house and our discussions were conducted in the hallway. So I decided I should mention the flying footstool and shoes.

'I was called because a neighbour felt something was wrong, that someone was in danger,' I told them.

'Ah, the neighbour! Very protective as usual,' said Brendan.

'Might I guess who rang you?' Avis put in. 'Miss Anson, was it?'

'I am not at liberty to say where our information came from.' I did not want them to go and attack Miss Anson! 'But clearly something has happened because when I arrived, I noticed a footstool on the lawn, near a pair of high-heeled shoes. And a large hole in one of your ground-floor windows.'

'That was me, Constable,' admitted Avis. 'It's nothing to worry about, the window pane was cracked and it needed a repair. By chance, I wanted rid of that old footstool, it's not fashionable any more. Those shoes were hurting so I got rid of them too. Nothing for anyone to be concerned about and certainly nothing to do with our neighbours. Or neighbour. I shall deal with them tomorrow. I'm sorry you have been involved like this.'

'I can soon have the window repaired, Officer,' put in Brendan. 'After all, I stock glass of all sizes, for domestic dwellings, offices and even greenhouses. I'll get a man to fix it. We haven't committed a crime, have we?'

'No,' I said. 'But if undue noise persists, your neighbours could take action through the local authority to reduce it or stop it completely.'

'Oh, we don't make a noise, Officer, we don't play loud music, or saw timber at night, or play the bagpipes or drums . . . we are just two happily married people enjoying ourselves, aren't we, darling?'

And she went to him, put her arms around his neck and planted a very sensuous kiss on his lips.

'There, Constable. We're friends and lovers, as you can see.' She smiled. 'And if I want to dispose of old furnishings and shoes by throwing them through the window, *my* window, I cannot see it is of any concern to anyone else. It seemed a good idea at the time. I'm sorry you have been troubled.'

'Well, so long as no one is hurt . . .'

'I would never hurt my darling wife, Officer, never.'

'And I would never hurt Brendan either.'

At this stage I decided I should do something to justify my presence. 'Well, I have to warn you to keep the noise down and not alarm your friends and neighbours . . . You know about the Noise Abatement Act of 1960? The council is quite determined to cut down domestic noise nuisances. You could be penalized if there are more complaints about your behaviour.'

'We'll both be very good!' they promised, but I pondered whether there would be further outbreaks of furniture

130

throwing and shouting. I felt it was for my benefit that they had staged a show of togetherness and I wondered what on earth had triggered the throwing spell and loud noises. Despite the pervading air of unnatural calm, I knew it was time to leave. I had absolutely no idea what had triggered their display of marital disharmony and there was nothing I could—or should—do. They could simply ask me to leave their home on the grounds that I was a trespasser so I let myself out. Julie Anson was still waiting outside.

'Are they all right?' she asked, with genuine concern.

'They look absolutely fine, smart and well dressed,' I told her. 'Not a hair out of place and both lovey-dovey. Avis said she was merely getting rid of the footstool and shoes . . . it's a weird way of getting rid of unwanted things and if they have had an almighty row they're very good at covering it up.'

'They are. It's always the same. I'm a friend of theirs, as I said earlier, and I worry about them. They always cover up their fights and next day they are as right as rain, all loving and caring and cuddling as if they have no cares in the world.'

'A stormy relationship. Blowing hot and then cold. Isn't that how some of these marriages are described?'

'A very stormy relationship in this case, Mr Rhea. You didn't hear the shouts and screams that I heard. I am used to their behaviour, but honestly this time I thought murder was being done, otherwise I wouldn't have called you.'

'I've warned them as to their future conduct.' I wanted her to know I had done something positive. 'That's our standard method of dealing with domestic dramas. I've also told them about the powers available to the local authority under the Noise Abatement Act of 1960. To avoid infringing that statute, I advised them to keep their noise down.'

'Isn't there any other kind of agency that can come and talk to them, help them to sort out their difficulties? Marital, I mean?'

'We can't offer help with marriage guidance or anything else; it is all down to them. If they want help of that kind, they must make the first approach. It is not a matter for the police.'

'I suppose it's nothing to do with any of us. Well, I suppose that's it until next time. So, when did you arrive in this area, PC Rhea?'

'It's a few months now, but this is the first time I've been called to this house.'

'It's not the first time for them, and it won't be the last.' She thanked me before returning to her own peaceful home which was all in darkness. I drove back to Ashfordly Police Station to write up my notes and booked off duty at 2 a.m. and returned to my own very peaceful home with no further incidents that night. But, as I lay in bed, my mind kept returning to the Connings as I struggled to understand their way of life despite knowing it had nothing whatever to do with me or my duties.

As I lay awake, I knew there was something not quite right about the situation I had just witnessed. It was rather like examining the scene of a serious crime—I knew there was something I should have noticed, but I had missed it. I had missed something crucial and because I pondered in my wakefulness, it was very late when eventually I fell asleep. In spite of my restlessness, I was up next morning at eight o'clock because the children were running around prior to heading off to school. I could not have slept late anyway because I was scheduled to be on duty at 10 a.m. for a tour of my own beat. I helped Mary with the breakfast and washing-up, then she took the children off to school as I prepared for my own tour of duty.

When she returned, I was working in the little office attached to my police house, preparing my day's schedule of visits, when Mary said, 'I could do with a coffee now they're at school. How about you, Nick?'

'That'll just set me up before I go on patrol.'

I must have sounded very weary because she asked, 'Are you all right?'

'Fine as I can be after a two-thirty finish! It's like having a hangover after a party. I took ages to get to sleep last night.'

'Well, at least you'll finish at six tonight and we can have an early night, unless you get called out!' and off she went to make the coffee. She brought it into my office and joined me at my desk.

'So, did you have a busy night?' she asked. 'You do seem under-the-weather, or is it just tiredness? Or is there a problem of some kind?'

'Tiredness, I think.' I told her all about the Connings and the long-running reports of their disruptive behaviour that was upsetting the neighbours while leaving the police powerless to take any kind of preventive action. I told her that my mind could not detach itself from their behaviour, or the associated circumstances and so I had been late getting to sleep.

'That's unusual for you! Nothing seems to bother you once your head hits the pillow.'

'I don't normally let things get to me, but this couple are so lovely, so charming, so successful and clearly so much in love even after thirty years, and yet they fight and throw things as if they are students at some kind of drug-induced rave. I could not understand how that woman could throw those things out of the window in anger and a few minutes later appear to be all sweetness and light with not a hair out of place. She must be a mighty good actress. But there is something not quite right about the whole affair. I am not sure what it is; I've missed something that should be very obvious to me.'

'It's called love, Nick; it's the way they behave.' She smiled in her knowing manner. 'Love can manifest itself in all kinds of ways. Some people can't live together no matter how much they love one another, but they can't live apart either. Perhaps the Connings should find a house with no neighbours, somewhere in the middle of a field where they could shout and fight and throw things to their hearts' content.'

'Their house is on its own, quite a long way from the neighbours and for some reason Miss Anson was genuinely worried about them,' I said. 'She honestly felt something

133

nasty would happen if they weren't stopped—and she could be right. I'm sure she knows them better than most, being a friend and neighbour.'

'Anyone would worry like that if there were lots of unexplained noises and shouting and things flying through the air at night.'

'It wasn't like any of the other domestics I've attended. I've seen dozens where couples have been at loggerheads, but none could appear as calm and normal as the Connings did, especially so soon after the event.'

'Maybe they knew the police had been called and were ready for you?'

'It's possible. According to Miss Anson, their rumpus worried the neighbours, not merely annoyed them. It was worry, Mary, not anger. That's why the whole affairs concerns me. I've heard all about their barneys, but I'd never met the couple in their home until last night.'

'Now you're an expert on family rows, are you?'

'You're not taking me seriously! I know I'm only a policeman and not a psychologist, but I do see life in all its colours and complexities, and this domestic incident was—and still is—very complex, if only in my humble opinion.'

'So what are you going to do?'

'What can I do? Nothing. I'll wait to see if it happens again.'

In an effort to understand the Connings' behaviour, each time I was on duty in either Ashfordly or Brantsford Police Offices, I would check the Occurrence Book to see whether there had been any more complaints about them. The Occurrence Book was a kind of desk diary maintained in every police station and in which every recorded local incident was noted, together with an account of the action taken. As I began to check previous dates, I noticed at least ten occasions when someone had telephoned to complain about the noise and damage at the Connings' house. In every case no action was taken because it had all happened within their home. There was no noticeable pattern—the outbreaks had occurred at different times during the week, not mainly on Friday or Saturday nights, the traditional time for marital flare-ups. In all instances, the Connings had been warned as to their future conduct even if there was no evidence of a serious domestic dispute when the police arrived—and the incidents continued.

From time to time, I patrolled Graindale as our beats expanded to include more villages. Due to the constant grumbles about the Connings I always made a point of walking around the group of pretty thatched cottages that surrounded theirs, particularly if it was in the late evening, but I never came across any trouble. Once or twice, I noticed Miss Anson working in her garden and always asked, 'All quiet, is it?'

'At the moment, yes, Mr Rhea. We have had our moments from time to time; I haven't always alerted the police; it's only when things seem to be getting dangerously out of hand. As I told you before, I'm a family friend but there are times I worry about the outcome.'

I assured her that she was doing the right thing in reporting any major outbreaks of violent trouble due to the likelihood of injury to one or other of the parties. I assured her that her motives for informing the police were sound. That seemed to please her.

For a comparatively long period afterwards, there seemed to be no reports of alarming activities within the Connings' household. That belief was strengthened in my mind because neither of the Occurrence Books at Ashfordly and Brantsford carried reports of recent trouble. I began to think they had overcome whatever problem had been at the root of their bizarre behaviour. Then, one Sunday morning, I was on a foot patrol of Ashfordly town centre. It was during the summer when the little town was overwhelmed with cars and tourists and my immediate task was to keep traffic moving and to prevent troublesome parking.

I was also responsible for patrolling the rest of the town if my commitments permitted. My patrol began at 10 a.m. and finished at 2 p.m. when another officer would take my place.

I would then return to my own beat at Aidensfield. I was making a point at the telephone kiosk in Ashfordly market-place, a device we used if any duty officers in local police stations needed to contact us. They would ring us on the public phone. It was shortly after eleven o'clock and both the Catholic and Anglican parish churches were turning out when I spotted Brendan Conning marching across the market-square towards his car. He spotted me and waved, then headed towards me.

'Ah, PC Rhea, and how are you this fine Sunday morning?'

'Fine thanks, just doing my bit to keep the town moving and the tourists happy.'

'That seems to be your mission in life, keeping people happy! I was sorry you were called to our house the other week. It's been getting a bit hectic lately with all those complaints and more than a little embarrassing, but she's calmed down a lot since you called.'

'She?' I thought he was referring to his wife but wanted to be sure. He'd referred to her only as 'she'.

'Miss Anson. Julie. You might have realized she's behind all this, constantly making malicious complaints, calling out the police to all sorts of fictitious incidents involving us. I know we've built up an awful reputation among your officers thanks to her, but what can we do? She claims to be a friend, but she's not, Mr Rhea, never has been. We never let her into our house.'

'I had no idea she was a troublemaker, Mr Conning. That isn't in our records. Most of the calls were anonymous and went to different police stations or police houses.'

'You've every reason not to believe me, but that's how it is. She is the only person who calls out the police and gets them to come to our house on a pretext that we're having a fight, or making too much noise. I know you have to act if you get reports, but I don't think your officers realize all this. We get a different officer each time . . . how can they know what lies behind it all? I am sure you don't have meetings to discuss my marital problems! And how can they prove she's making the calls?'

'Have you told anyone about this? Your solicitor?'

'No, to be honest, we feel sorry for the woman even if she is a pest.'

'Perhaps she is ill?'

'Maybe PC Rhea. Perhaps something mental, but I dare not suggest such a thing to her, but I do think she is not fully *compos mentis* if you understand. She behaves stupidly from time to time and can be very trying.' He paused and looked at me very steadily for a second or two as if trying to make up his mind about something else he wanted to say, then said, 'I've seen you at mass, have I not? In St Mary's here at Ashfordly and sometimes at St Aidan's in Aidensfield?'

'Yes, I attend both. I am a Catholic.'

'Me, too. And for that reason, I will trust you, Mr Rhea. Perhaps you could call at the house sometime when you are in the area? I'm home most evenings and Sundays. There's something I would like to discuss that is relevant to this matter and I don't feel it is a matter for the parish priest. A trusty policeman would be far better, but not here in the market-place where ears might be flapping!'

'All right, I'll come along.' I wondered what on earth he could want to discuss with me. And then I heard the telephone ringing in the nearby kiosk.

'I must go, Mr Conning, that will be for me. I will call on you, I promise.'

'Just drop in if you're in the area.' He strode over to his car as I picked up the phone. 'Weekends or evenings are best.'

'Nick, get yourself down to the Connings' house in Graindale, there's a fire,' it was PC Rogers from Eltering. 'The brigade has been called.'

'Right!'

I didn't waste time asking questions but rushed out of the kiosk and was in time to hail Mr Conning as he was preparing to drive away. He saw me racing towards his car and waving my arms, so he opened the driver's door to talk to me.

'That was our Eltering office, Mr Conning, there's a fire at your house. I have to get there . . .'

'Jump in, for God's sake.'

'Forget any speed limits!' I said, as we roared out of the market-place.

'What sort of fire? Not the thatch, is it?'

'They didn't say.'

'She wouldn't do that, set fire to anything. I know she wouldn't, she's not that bad,' he said, as we roared along.

'The thatch is safe is it, from catching fire?'

'As safe as it can be . . . Holy Mother of God, I wonder what she's done now.'

We didn't speak during the short journey, each sitting with our own thoughts, but as he turned into Graindale from the main road, I could see a plume of smoke rising from the thatched houses. When we turned into the close, the smoke was rising from the garden of the Connings' house as a fire appliance stood by, idly.

I rushed out of the car with Brendan at my side and saw it was a pile of garden materials—dead grass, tree branches, cuttings, flowers and even some pieces of woodwork like old fencing. I noticed the footstool among the wood. Avis was there wearing a head-square and poking at the smouldering heap with a garden hoe. She was stirring it up, trying to encourage the material to burst into flames. But much of it was too green and damp, producing a lot of smoke. As Brendan rushed over to Avis, I went to the fire appliance, the formal name for a fire engine, and spoke to the crew.

'So what's the story?' There were four men sitting in the cab.

'999 call, fire at this address. So here we are. That's the only fire we can find; it's not affecting the house but we're keeping an eye on that woman who is trying to stoke up the flames. She's the householder burning garden rubbish, so she says, but we don't want any of that thatch going up.'

'It looks safe enough to me, far enough from all the thatched cottages.'

'The woman who rang said she was sure the thatch was on fire, and I must admit it did look like that from a certain angle. She did right; we're not complaining about her actions so it was a false call-out with good intent. A useful exercise for us, certainly not a waste of time. We'll wait until we are sure there's no likelihood of any damage.'

A small crowd had gathered to watch the excitement and I spotted Miss Anson chatting to some of them.

I wondered if she had made the alarm call, but if she had, her name would be in the fire service records, unless she had given false particulars. I would not quiz her at this stage because no offence had been committed. I must admit I began to wonder at Mr Conning's statement that she was a busybody and not a genuine friend of the Connings. As Avis was stoking up the bonfire, Brendan came over to me.

'Another storm in a tea-cup,' he said. 'Avis is just burning garden rubbish. She's not a Catholic by the way; she doesn't go to church with me. Some busybody rang the Fire Brigade. I wonder who? Have we have an enemy in our midst?' And he smiled wryly.

'The brigade said they were told the fire was in the thatch, or it looked as if it was, which is why they turned out.'

'Could be. Their fire engine can sit there as long as it wants, but the house is safe and not at risk. Avis is going to come in now, so you must come in too, Mr Rhea, and have a coffee with us. I would like you to meet Avis in more genial circumstances than your earlier visit. You got here rather sooner than I expected thanks to this fire! It's the perfect time to talk, then I'll run you back to Ashfordly.'

I was suddenly aware of our old police advice that we should never take sides during a domestic dispute, but I felt a mere coffee would not be a problem. In any case, I wanted to hear the Connings' side of what was clearly a long and involved story and I hoped our chat would put my mind at rest. Brendan said Avis would take orders from the firemen, who could not leave their post for some time, and so he led me into the kitchen where there was a large table, an Aga and some comfortable chairs. We could watch the action from here, so it was a wise choice. I could see Miss Anson standing alone observing the progress.

Without speaking for a while, Brendan busied himself putting the kettle on the Aga and organized some mugs, milk and sugar as Avis remained outside to deal with requests from the firemen.

'I'm not inviting the neighbours in.' He grinned at me. 'They might ring the police . . .'

'Miss Anson you mean?'

'Aye, she's a troublemaker all right, Mr Rhea. She rings the police at the least provocation, always claiming we are fighting and scrapping and shouting. I bet she rang the brigade today—it's like those people who harass personalities or film stars. She won't leave us alone.'

'I can check to see whether she did ring,' I promised him.

'I wish you would.'

And then Avis walked in. She smelt of smoke and was covered in bits of scorched grass and leaves but she smiled when she saw me. Brendan explained my presence, and that of the Fire Brigade, and she sighed. 'Not our so-called friend and neighbour again, was it?'

'PC Rhea can check. I have explained things to him.'

'But not everything?'

'No. I saw him in Ashfordly just as he got the call to come here, I invited him to come in for a chat next time he was passing. He's got here sooner than I expected!'

'Mr Rhea,' said Avis, 'you must think we are awful, those reports, those police visits. And all because a woman can't stop poking her nose into our business. Yes, we do argue. Brendan is a Catholic and I'm a Protestant; we argue about religion and our voices get raised but it's all good-natured . . . but that footstool and shoes, well, I did it deliberately to give Miss Anson something to think about.'

'A bit of fun, you mean?'

'Yes, but only to be sure it was she who was calling the police at the least sign of raised voices or music or something in our house. We wanted to know who was behind all those police visits. We've staged one or two events to get the necessary proof. This time, that window pane was cracked and Brendan said he would fix it with some glass from the shop, so for a bit of fun with Julie Anson, I threw that old footstool through it when we knew she was prowling around the garden, and followed it with a pair of unwanted shoes.'

'I built the bonfire a few days ago,' said Brendan. 'I've been clearing out a lot of rubbish from my garage and outbuildings and stacked it near my rubbish tip, ready for disposal. Old chairs, a settee, a couple of tables, an old wardrobe . . . when the police came before because someone said we were throwing chairs about, that's what I showed them. It was malicious gossip, Mr Rhea. Your records don't show that?'

'Not in Ashfordly, Mr Conning. But thanks for telling me.'

'But now we know who the caller is—Miss Julie Anson.'

'So why is she doing this?' I asked. 'It sounds like a vendetta to me.'

'It's because she loves him, Mr Rhea,' said Avis, placing coffee mugs before us. 'She has a fixation for Brendan. She's trying all the time to attract his attention; she needs treatment, believe me. We know she comes into our garden at night, prowling around and hoping to catch a glimpse of him through the windows, so she might hear us playing music or listening to a television drama. She fell in love with Brendan at a distance, but that was some years ago when he was a single man making his way in the world. She has chased him ever since: she's even come to live next door . . . so what can we do? I don't want to have her locked up or put into a mental home, and I admit we do lead her on sometimes, just to prove it's her.'

'Like putting out a window that was broken anyway?'

'Yes, that sort of thing. She always reacts; I don't think she realizes what she's doing. It's all very sad. But I do wish we could stop her.'

I thought a moment. 'I think I will go and obtain a written statement from her, outlining all her recent complaints including your garden fire. Then I'll point out that if she says anything in the statement that is untrue, it will amount to perjury. That might stop her. And, of course, I'll make sure all our officers at Eltering, Brantsford and Ashfordly are aware of her campaign against you. If she persists, we could get her bound over to be of good behaviour in court which would mean she must cease her harassment. But I will need sound evidence that she is responsible.'

'I think she has used false names sometimes, or just not said who was calling. The police and fire officers have told me that, they check the source of such calls. We have had the brigade out before, to a false alarm or two. You might find they have a record of it all. One officer dropped such a hint, but I could not make a formal complaint against her because I lacked any real evidence. And the senior police officers would not make an enquiry on my behalf because I lacked evidence. They can't trace the phone calls once the handset's been replaced. They told me to see a solicitor and deal with it as a civil matter.'

'Let's hope we can get the matter sorted out for you. I'll start a little investigation of my own,' I told them. 'And I'll keep you informed.'

I now knew why I had been unsettled about this series of events. The Connings had appeared to be loving and calm upon the arrival of the police quite simply because Miss Anson had invented the stories of fights and violence. There had been no such fights or violence. The Connings were calm folk, even if they had launched their footstool-throwing diversion for the benefit of Miss Anson.

Later, I checked in considerable detail all our records for complaints against the Connings and several had openly been made by Miss Julie Anson from the telephone in her home. There were also many anonymous calls that were untraceable. She had not had the wit to make use of public telephone kiosks every time in her mad campaign. Somehow, through

142

the simple action of repeatedly calling the police but making her calls to different police stations and talking to several different officers or even the Fire Brigade, Miss Anson had managed to create an aura of disrepute about the Connings, Avis in particular. I felt she was jealous of Avia for marrying Brendan.

After my careful search of all our records, I went to interview Miss Anson about her complaints and asked that she make a long written statement outlining the reason for every one of her actions while reminding her that any false allegations could result in a charge of perjury. There was also the matter of making malicious telephone calls. I told her that repeated harassment of another person could be dealt with as 'conduct likely to cause a breach of the peace', a matter that could end with fines or imprisonment.

We received no more complaints about the behaviour of Mr and Mrs Connings and Miss Anson soon moved from the area. She went to live in Scarborough and so I rang Scarborough Police to alert them to the arrival in their patch of a persistent complainer. I felt that this had been an eavesdropping case with everything not being fair in love and war.

7. FAYRE'S FAIR

When I was considering taking up an interest other than my work and family, I decided to examine the detailed history and lore of Aidensfield and district. I soon discovered that the more I delved into the past, the more engrossing it became. One of the little-known facts that emerged was that the original parish church had been built in Saxon times long before the Church of England had been established, and it had been dedicated to St Aidan. He was a noted saint and missionary who lived on the island of Lindisfarne off the Northumbrian coast. That ancient Aidensfield church had been in a poor state of repair long before being reconstructed on the same site in 1456 by using much of the original stone.

Around a century later, as a consequence of the Reformation, that second church was destroyed. Its stones, font, statues and other sacred objects were scattered across the moors or sold to merchants. Its ancient site was oblite-rated. That was effected by government officials who paid contractors to carry out the work because the congregation had refused to conform to the Protestant reformed Church of England. They insisted on following their historic Catholic faith that had become known as 'the old religion' or 'papism'. For many years, therefore, Aidensfield did not have a church of any kind and the Anglicans made use of the parish church at Elsinby. In Victorian times, however, a new Protestant parish church was built in Aidensfield and dedicated to All Saints, but it did not occupy the site of that former Catholic building. It was constructed on the western edge of the village green and is still in use today. With the passage of time, the exact location of both St Aidan's old Catholic churches had become uncertain because references to them had been deleted from local history books. It was as if the old faith's Catholic church had never existed. However, the concealed aspects of its history began emerge in the 1960s and later. This generated a great deal of speculation among Catholics who had moved into the village. Quite simply, there was no sign of the building and, more surprisingly, no sign of its graveyard. Local folklore suggested that after the Reformation, even the tombstones and the churchyard cross had been removed and smashed into pieces to be later used in the construction of houses or other structures in the district. It was not unknown for an old tombstone to end its life as a paving stone or part of a house, albeit with any portion of the inscription being concealed within the wall.

In spite of that traumatic period of the sixteenth and seventeenth centuries, the name of St Aidan lives on in the only English village that bears his name despite the main area of his missionary work being much further north in what is now Northumberland. Although Aidan's missionary work took him all over the north-east of England, he did not attend the famous Synod of Whitby (perhaps more accurately called the Synod of Streonshalh) in AD 664 simply because he had died a few years earlier in either AD 626 or 641. The precise date of his death is uncertain.

Whether or not he ever visited Aidensfield has not been confirmed, but there is a legend that he passed through the village. As a result of that visit, the community become known as Adenesfelt—in other words it was the predecessor of Aidensfield. During his visit, he was said to have celebrated mass and preached to the people who were assembled in a field on the edge of the village. During the service, he prodded that field with his stave whereupon a spring of water appeared. A well was constructed over the spring and local legend says it has never run dry even in the most severe of droughts. Furthermore, its waters were said to cure any ailment in man and beast. The water from St Aidan's Well is still used to fill the flower vases in both the Catholic and Anglican churches, and is also used in the fonts and piscinas.

Not surprisingly, the incident of the well led to the field becoming known as Aidan's Field. Over the years, the spelling of Aidan was changed to Aiden with an 'e' when it was incorporated in the village name. With no church to call their own, the Aidensfield Catholics originally met in houses and celebrated Holy Mass in barns and stables until a new Roman Catholic chapel was built in 1790. A stained-glass window depicting St Aidan standing alongside the other famous northern saints, Cuthbert and Hilda, was especially commissioned in 1848. The church, with other modifications, now stands to the west of the village almost within sight of the Anglican Church, with the colourful window of the Three Saints prominent behind the altar.

It is almost certain that the present St Aidan's does not occupy the site of the former Saxon church but the possibility has never been discounted. If it does occupy that site, it is due to pure coincidence rather than careful planning. However, research by a local historian from ancient documents recently discovered in an old house proved that Aidan's Field is actually owned by the ancient Catholic parish of Aidensfield and this has led to much speculation that the field may have been the former graveyard of the Saxon church and its medieval successor. But no bones or signs of human burial have been found, the ancient cross has never been located and it is known that the gravestones were removed and recycled.

Naturally, in trying to discover more details of Aidensfield's early history I would have been excited to be able to confirm the site of the original church. I have always felt that a location on or near Aidan's Field was the most likely place. If that field had been the churchyard or burial ground, then the church would almost certainly have stood on the site. In my lengthy quest, I delved into all kinds of ancient records, letters, documents and maps instead of accepting the rather bland versions presented in standard history books. However, while not discovering the origins of the village's first church, I learned that the field had been the site of an old fair. It was known as St Aidan's Churchyard Fair and it was always held on his feast day which was 31 August.

The fact that the churchyard fair had been held in that field provided strong evidence that it had once been the churchyard. That being so, burials would have also taken place there and there would probably have been a churchyard cross—the purpose of that cross was to symbolize the Catholic faith over the graves of those whose families could not afford their own memorials.

Events such as markets and fairs were held in churchyards long before the Reformation. Fairs were often on the feast day of the patron saint of the parish church when the whole village made it a holiday, the name 'holiday' coming from holy day.

Before the Protestant Reformation, a village church of the old religion was the focus of the community with social events such as fairs, markets and other gatherings being held either inside the building, usually within the nave, or alternatively within its grounds. Those grounds would be large enough to accommodate public events without interfering with the section set aside for burials—there was space for all the parishioners, dead or alive. Almost every celebratory event of this kind would be preceded by Holy Mass. Celebration of the feast day of the village's patron saint was always a very joyful occasion and because it was a parish holiday it was usually accompanied by music, drink, feasting and dancing. Obviously some misbehaviour occurred which is probably why the practice of holding such events on holy ground came to an end.

One peculiarity that I discovered was that in art, the emblem of St Aidan was a stag, probably a red deer, which roamed the northern hills and forests. As part of the St Aidan's Day celebrations, a dance was performed by men wearing stags' antlers, rather like some Morris dances. The precise symbolism of the antlers was never made clear.

Morris dancing and sword dancing were also held in the nave of the church and sometimes it hosted mystery plays and other social events. The church therefore served an important dual purpose—entertainment and education. Children would also be taught in church by using the statues and wall paintings to illustrate various aspects of the gospel—but these were ripped out and destroyed during the Reformation in the mistaken belief they were idolatrous, or some form of pagan symbolism. There were no seats in the naves at that time, the congregation remaining standing throughout the mass, although some stone pews were fitted around the walls to provide places of rest for the elderly and infirm. Many of those wall-seats survive to this day in churches dating from the so-called old religion.

Before the Reformation the interiors of parish churches were very colourful and richly decorated with monuments and statues, rood lofts, tabernacles and wall paintings. Fanatical reformers tore them down and threw them out, or alternatively sold sacred objects to merchants and dealers as mere ornamentation. The bare church was then used for Protestant services, or alternatively destroyed. It was a dreadful period of English history. The most important result of my research, however, was the knowledge that for centuries a churchyard fair had been held on St Aidan's Field annually on 31 August.

The celebrations included eating, drinking, music and dancing. It was quite humbling to realize that the field containing St Aidan's Well had been used for those celebrations and that his well was still flowing after more than 1300 years. As I continued to delve into ancient records and quiz the older people about their own memories, or about legends passed down to them by their ancestors, I learned that the churchyard fair had been established by royal charter in

1476. It had been held on that field until 1913, even though its parent church had been destroyed.

Throughout that time it continued to be known as St Aidan's Churchyard Fair and it had attracted people from all over the moors as produce and livestock was bought and sold, dancing was enjoyed, games were held and plays were produced all to the happy sounds of local musicians. And it was all in honour of their patron saint. It was a thriving example of what occurred during the days of Merrie England. Entertainment of the kind had been forbidden during the Protestant Reformation on the grounds it was too pagan, or laced with superstition, but the fair revived briefly in the nineteenth century, only to dwindle away during World War I because so many local men were overseas fighting for their country. Brief efforts to revive it in 1944 also failed because World War II had come along to intervene and it was never staged after that conflict.

In reading its history, I wondered if it would be possible to revive the ancient fair on that very same field, albeit in a modern format. The current St Aidan's Church was urgently in need of funds to repair the roof and the revival of its own special summertime fair, supported by lots of history and, hopefully, lots of people, seemed an ideal means of raising some of the necessary cash. I decided to float the idea with the Catholic parish priest. His name was Father Simon. Father Simon was a Benedictine monk of Maddleskirk Abbey, a busy monastery about two miles from Aidensfield, who had been charged with the duty of caring for Aidensfield parish. I never knew his surname—all the monks were known by their first names. A small, slightly built man in his late fifties, he had a mop of thick dark air and rather elfin-like features that were made cheerful by a perpetual smile. I could imagine him once being a freckled-faced lad who was always getting into mischief. However, he was a noted mathematician and author of several text-books on that subject. His studious manner was emphasized by heavy, horn-rimmed spectacles that perched on the end of his nose and, when not clad in

149

his monk's habit or priest's robes, he loved to wear old civilian clothes that made him look like a gardener or a farm labourer. In that guise, he spent hours working in the garden and grounds that surrounded the church so the exterior of St Aidan's was always immaculate.

I was patrolling past the church one Monday morning in February and spotted him pruning some roses; it was not a full pruning session but one designed to help the plants cope with the forthcoming severity of the March winds.

'Father Simon,' I hailed him. 'Good to see you so busy.'

'I'm not sure I am doing the right thing to these roses.' He straightened up to speak to me. 'I'm sure a real gardener would say it is the wrong time of year and not the correct way to prune them, but they are rather exposed on that corner and catch a lot of wind. I've seen branches whipped about by strong winds and sometimes snapped off.'

'I leave all that kind of thing to my wife; she's the expert in our house.'

'I have volunteers who sometimes turn up, but not always when they are wanted! So there are times I must do it myself.'

'I know you're very busy, but there's an idea I'd like to suggest,' I put to him. 'It could be a means of raising money for the church roof.'

'Well, I'm always keen to hear suggestions of that kind; the roof is becoming a major problem, Nick. Come in and let me hear your ideas.'

He led me into the tiny vestry at the back of the church where there were two chairs at each end of a very small table, and upon which sat a kettle and some mugs.

'Coffee?' he asked. 'I always have a coffee about now, which is why I have arranged my own very sparse little kitchen. Otherwise, I'd have to return to the monastery every time I fancied a drink and that is not really feasible.'

As he boiled the kettle and prepared our drinks, he asked about my family and chattered about village matters, then sat down opposite as he presented me with my coffee.

'So, what is this idea of yours, Nick?'

'I've been doing some research into St Aidan's Field and came across a reference to the churchyard fair—you'll probably know all about it—and I've discovered it was held every year in that field on his feast day, 31 August.'

'Yes, I do know of the old fair, but I've never associated it with that field. Amazing! But it's odd you should call now—do you know Mrs Lambert, Rebecca Lambert? She lives in Ferncliffe Cottage. A retired school secretary, a widow too. Her husband died before she came to live here. I must tell you that she has already got things moving to revive the fair so the idea is not new. And I think she is hoping to use that field, even if she does not know its full history.'

'Oh,' I said, with perhaps a suggestion of disappointment at having been pipped at the proverbial post. I went on, 'I've seen her around the village and, of course, at mass, but we're not really acquainted.'

She was a very tall woman with ruddy cheeks and thick grey hair. She had a loud voice and a propensity for dressing in tweed skirts and woollen jumpers. She was the sort of person who would never be ignored wherever she went. Since coming to live in Aidensfield about two years ago, she had involved herself in most of the organizations where her secretarial skills had proved invaluable and where her strong personality had led to her selection as chairman or president of a number of local committees.

'Well, I think your researches around the village during the past few months must have set people thinking, Nick, because she came to see me after mass last Sunday with exactly the same idea as you. She thinks we should revive the St Aidan's Churchyard Fair to make money for our roof repair fund.'

'That's wonderful news! So, is she doing anything about it?'

'She said she would ask around the village with a special emphasis upon members of our congregation, to see if she could drum up any interest and support for the idea. If she gets a positive response, she can't do the job on her own, Nick, so she'll need a committee. She's good at that. She'll see that she's appointed chairman and will put herself in full charge of all the arrangements. Does that bother you? It's your initiative too . . .'

'No, I've no problem with someone else doing the arrangements. It's never easy getting involved in something like this because of my police commitments—I can never foresee when I shall be called out to an incident of some kind, or have to attend court or stand-in for another constable who has become ill . . .'

'I understand; it's similar within the priesthood so I think such arrangements are best left to retired people who need to occupy themselves with something worthwhile. Like Mrs Lambert.'

'And you would be in favour of the idea?'

'Of course, the abbey will help us if the roof becomes unstable, but in the meantime, we have to make our own efforts. If we can't raise enough for the roof repairs, then the abbey will make up the difference—but the procurator has told me in no uncertain terms, that he expects us to raise some funds. So this idea from two of my parishioners at the same time is most fortuitous.'

'I'll go and see Mrs Lambert,' I promised.

'She'll give you a job!' he laughed. 'And you'll find yourself on the committee! She's already persuaded me to be treasurer for the event.'

And so it was that later that day I knocked on the door of Ferncliffe Cottage with its lovely white woodwork, red pantile roof and mellow stonework.

'Oh dear, the policeman!' Mrs Lambert shrank back in dismay when she saw me at the door. 'Has something awful happened?'

'Not to my knowledge!' That kind of response happened almost every occasion a uniformed police officer knocked unexpectedly on someone's door. In truth it often heralded bad news but not on this occasion. As I began to explain my mission, she smiled with relief and invited me in with the offer of a piece of cake and a cup of tea. That was traditional in most villages—everyone who called was made welcome in that way.

'Well, Mr Rhea, this is a surprise. So you're interested in reviving St Aidan's Churchyard Fair?'

She bade me sit on one of her armchairs as I explained about my researches. She acknowledged that she had heard of my efforts through other people whom I had approached in Aidensfield for their memories or old records or letters, and she was full of enthusiasm for a revival.

'We need to create the atmosphere of Merrie England,' she beamed. 'Lots of colour, music, happiness and fun.'

'My idea completely!' I enthused.

She seemed happy that she had found a fellow enthusiast. 'I'm not saying we should revive jousting or archery contests or anything dangerous, but I believe that if we are to recreate this fair as near as possible to its original format, we need to involve as many local craftsmen and women as we can. We also need to attract local businesses, manufacturers, experts of every kind, sport, competitions, children's events, music, dancing and so forth. And I see no reason why we should not have a bar too . . . that would be legal, wouldn't it?'

I explained that the liquor licensing laws allowed bars to function at events that were held away from licensed premises, albeit with certain rules and guidelines. I added that George Ward, landlord of the Brewers Arms in Aidensfield, would be pleased to arrange the necessary facilities and that pleased her—she would contact him, she said. We discussed the kind of stalls and activities that we felt would be essential to making the fair a success, all of which could be secured from people living within the Aidensfield district, and then she said, 'Well, Mr Rhea, I think we are agreed the idea is feasible with some hard work and a little bit of luck. I have already made some approaches to people who can help, but we'll have to work quickly because it is now February and it must be held on 31

August, St Aidan's feast day, in his very own field. That is the entire purpose of the revived fair. It may seem a long way off but time flashes past with astonishing speed.'

At that time, of course, prior to 1967, the August bank holiday was celebrated on the first Monday of that month, not the last Monday as it has been since 1967 and so we could not take advantage of the holiday atmosphere to generate a crowd. We would have to do our best without it. As we chatted, I could sense she was fired up with enthusiasm and I did not therefore volunteer to become the organizer, chairman or secretary of the committee, adding only, 'Well, if I can be of any help—'

'You can, Mr Rhea, there is no doubt about it. I am already in the throes of forming a committee that will make the necessary arrangements and they will organize the format of the day.'

'You've moved very fast!'

'One cannot allow grass to grow beneath one's feet, Mr Rhea, when there are decisions to be made and things to be organized. I shall make one person responsible for each of certain components of the day—sports, children's events, flower and vegetable stalls, craft stalls, food stalls, music and dancing, catering and everything else that is a vital part of an event of this kind.'

'I like your style, Mrs Lambert!'

'It comes from years of experience, Mr Rhea. I've lost count of the number of village fêtes I organized before moving to Aidensfield. I was president of the local WI, president of the Catholic Women's League, chairman of school governors, secretary of the village hall committee . . . you name it, Mr Rhea, and I have always held an executive position. I will love arranging this fair, it won't be difficult and it will enable me to do my bit for our church. After all, I am retired with plenty of time on my hands, not to mention years of acquiring the necessary skills and experience.'

'My duties make it difficult for me to devote my time to matters where regular meetings are expected,' I tried to explain. 'I find myself having to cancel things at the last minute when I get called out to an incident, even something basic like a traffic accident or reported theft.'

'Say no more, Mr Rhea. I shall see to everything. Now, we need to drum up support in the whole village, not only from St Aidan's but also from the Methodists and Anglicans and, of course, those who do not profess any faith. I would consider it a great privilege to have you on the committee because of your legal expertise and your knowledge of the district.'

'That's no problem, even if I can't promise to attend every one.'

'Good. I am sure there are rules and regulations that affect such events and we must not infringe the law. Of course, you'd be most welcome as a member of the committee, and we hope you can attend on the day itself, if only because of your car-parking skills.'

'I'll help in any way I can. There are occasions when we are allowed to attend such committee meetings as part of our police duty, if there is no other pressing matter. The chief constable likes village constables to take part in all community matters even in those not directly associated with the police. So I might turn up in uniform from time to time— I'll make sure the sergeant and officers at Ashfordly Police Station know where to find me if I'm needed.'

'That is a very enlightened outlook, Mr Rhea. I look forward to working with you.'

And so, after discussing one or two very minor details, I left her and returned to Father Simon in his garden to explain how Mrs Lambert was organizing the churchyard fair with her traditional gusto. I stressed her wish that help and support would be needed both now and on the great day.

'I'll mention it to our congregation,' he promised. 'They're very good at buckling down to work of that kind, and I know they and their families will give us every ounce of support. Thanks, Nick.'

As the days and weeks passed, we began to receive positive commitments. Word of the forthcoming fair had circulated to those who constantly sought a platform to sell their goods and wares, and part of St Aidan's Field had been earmarked for children's athletics and some adult competitions including a twenty-over cricket match. We received a good response from organizations that wished only to advertise their services such as the National Farmers' Union, the Prudential Assurance Association, the Red Cross, the Royal Automobile Club and even the recruiting departments of local police forces, the RAF, the Army and the Royal Navy. What had begun as an idea in someone's mind was now taking shape in a way that exceeded our expectations.

And then, as the day of the fair drew closer, I spotted an advertisement on the parish noticeboard in Aidensfield. It announced the date and venue of St Aidan's Fayre on Wednesday, 31 August commencing at noon on St Aidan's Field. It included a condensed itinerary of the day's events. I was concerned because I knew there was no such word as fayre and felt some people might object to this frequently used corruption of the English language.

Fayre meant a fairy, but this word was not linked to fairies. I went home to check my assumption in various dictionaries, legal and otherwise but found only one reference to 'fayre' which said it was not a genuine word and was not in general use. It was used only on some occasions. It added that it was not an archaic word either. In other words it was an invented or fake word that was supposed to provide a medieval impression of the occasion. In the opinions of many, it did just the opposite—it looked cheap and contrived and I knew that a lot of educated people disliked its use. I am not an expert on the English language, although I am fairly knowledgeable about our local dialect, and I was aware that instances can occur where a new dialect word or even a new word in mainstream English is introduced to the language to later become standard. After all, that is how our language develops—consider new words like television, email, websites and so forth.

During the 1960s, fayre had not entered our standard dictionaries so I wondered whether or not to mention it to Mrs

Lambert in her capacity as the organizer. My own instinct was to allow the word to continue in use because the day of the fair was fast approaching and we needed as much publicity as we could generate. Furthermore, if we took down those posters, we would have to print some new ones and that would take time and add to the expenditure, with a corresponding reduction in our profits. Besides, I told myself, a lot of people honestly believed that 'fayre' was the correct name for an occasion of this kind. Eventually I convinced myself it was a harmless error and, as we say in North Yorkshire, I would 'say nowt about it'.

However, a few days later I met Mrs Lambert in the post office.

'How are things going with the fair?' I asked as we queued for postal orders and stamps.

'Wonderful,' she beamed. 'We have attracted lots of interest with commitments for plenty of stalls and side-shows. I am sure St Aidan's Field will be full to capacity, and the fees they will pay will go a long way towards our roof repairs. All we need now is a large crowd of fair-lovers who are not afraid of spending money.'

'Wednesday isn't perhaps the best day for an event like this, is it?' I pondered. 'Saturday is the usual day for fairs and shows when the schools are closed and people are looking for something different to occupy them over the weekend.'

'I did consider arranging it on the Saturday nearest to St Aidan's Day,' she said. 'But because it's a revival of an older fair, I thought it best to stick to the original date, the actual feast day for St Aidan, at least for the time being. Depending upon its success, we might change the date as suggested. I know Wednesday isn't the best day but, after all, businesses can give their staff time off. Besides, Wednesday afternoon is half-day closing in most shops and schoolchildren took reminders home before the holidays. The village people will turn up and tourists will be about.'

'Are you worried about a low attendance?' I put to her.

'Just a little, but I always am on these occasions,' she admitted. 'I must admit I've overheard people saying they can't attend because it's being held on a weekday instead of the weekend, and Jill Carver from the shop said the same. She'd overheard someone saying they couldn't attend because it's on a Wednesday.'

'But that's only two people!' I tried to be cheerful and positive.

'Yes, but it's a good indicator of the way people are thinking. Certainly we have excellent support from exhibitors, stallholders and some competitors who've promised to take part but success on the day depends on the turn-out of visitors.'

While chatting, I wondered whether I should refer to the use of 'fayre' but after a moment's reflection, I refrained. I hadn't heard anyone mention it and began to feel I was being unnecessarily pedantic. As I left the post office I tried to put the matter to the back of my mind, believing it would not make the slightest difference to the attendance figures. People would support the fair despite the peculiar name.

Then, on the Saturday morning preceding the fair, disaster struck Aidensfield. Someone had removed all the posters advertising the event, not only in Aidensfield but in the surrounding villages, including Ashfordly. It was Mrs Lambert who alerted me by calling at the police house just after nine o'clock as I was preparing for my day's duty. I was in my own small office, finalizing some paperwork before heading off to Ashfordly to check my in-tray.

'It's terrible, Mr Rhea. Who would do a thing like that? Why remove all our posters only days before the event? And when it's too late to get them reprinted . . .'

'Are you sure they've all gone?' I had to be sure about this. 'Could the wind have torn one or two down, or was it children misbehaving?'

'Oh yes, they've all been taken down, Mr Rhea. Quite deliberately. We can't blame children, or the wind and weather: it was a man.'

'How can you be sure?'

'Because Mrs Ford at Beck Cottage saw him, it was she who rang me. She was unable to sleep during the night and got up to make a cup of cocoa, and she saw him from her landing window. About two o'clock it was, and very dark except for the street lights. She saw him in the street lights.'

'So why would anyone do this? We've no rival fairs in the area, have we?'

'No, Mr Rhea. And I can't see it would be a religious battle either. I know there have been disputes about the ownership of the field, but that's all over now, the respective faiths tolerate one another. Anyway, after what she told me I went out this morning before eight o'clock and checked several sites where I had placed posters—the parish noticeboard, noticeboards at the two churches and the chapel, your own police noticeboard, several telegraph poles—all the outdoor sites. They've all been taken down, but posters are still showing inside the post office and shop—fortunately he couldn't touch those indoors at that time of night.'

'I must admit I hadn't noticed one was missing from the police noticeboard! I haven't ventured that far from home yet.'

'Well, it's gone, I can assure you of that, I've had a look.'

'So who is this man? Does Mrs Ford have any idea?'

'She wasn't sure who he was, I did ask, but I was rather more concerned with finding out whether her story was true. I didn't quiz her very closely about him. You might get more information from her. It is a very strange thing to do, Mr Rhea, whatever one's motive.'

'I'll go and see her straight away, Mrs Lambert. I'll try to get to the bottom of this and let you know what I discover.'

'So what do I do in the meantime, Mr Rhea? It's the weekend, we can't get new posters printed and this is the time we get visitors coming through, looking for something to do or somewhere to go . . .'

'Could you relocate some of the posters that have survived? Like those inside the post office, the pub, the shop and so forth? At least, it would be a presence on the street at this critical time, people passing through Aidensfield might see them.'

'Yes, yes, I'll do that and I can get some help. So, can you prosecute this man, Mr Rhea?'

'I can't recall any criminal offence that is committed by merely removing a poster but if he has destroyed them, then we might be able to charge him with malicious damage or even larceny if he has burnt them. If he removed them without authority and with an intention not to return them, then we could charge him with larceny, that's the word for stealing.'

'It is certainly a despicable thing to do, Mr Rhea. He needs to be caught and exposed for what he is.'

'I've got to find him first, then I need to talk to him to establish his motive.'

'Then I shall leave that in your capable hands as I try to salvage something from this disaster.'

And off she went as I prepared for my day's work. Mrs Ford was my first call, but before I left home I rang Ashfordly Police Station to book on duty. Sergeant Blaketon took the call. After booking on duty as required, I told him about the missing posters and he said, 'You'd better have a word with Alf Ventress, Nick. Recently he had to deal with a chap in Ashfordly who was going around correcting notices in shops where people had placed an apostrophe that wasn't in the right place. You know the sort of thing—plum's, pear's, bean's, pork pie's and even stamp's, book's and so forth. This chap was going around crossing them out with some correcting fluid or just rubbing them out if they were chalked on slates.'

'He'd be popular!' I laughed.

'He wasn't universally loved, I can tell you that. Some of the shopkeepers had deliberately included the apostrophes to attract the attention of shoppers who would then buy some of the goods in question. It's like those publicans who have notices saying "Bear Gardens" instead of "Beer Gardens". They always get someone calling in telling them of their mistake, but such people usually buy a drink or two.'

'But this man was taking down the posters,' I reminded him.

'Yes, you said that. The point I am making is that if a man was going around shops openly correcting spelling errors, he might be the sort of person who would take down a poster that was wrongly spelled or showing a wrong word. So were the posters misspelled? You'd better have words with Alf, he's here.'

After I explained, Alf said, 'Oh, yes, Nick. I remember him. He was from Aidensfield too. A retired freelance proof-reader, he worked for some of the big London publishers. He couldn't bear to see sloppy spelling and punctuation and so he wages a one-man campaign to make people aware of the correct use of language. He writes lots of letters to newspapers and magazines who get things wrong.'

'He's not making much impression, Alf, they still make those mistakes,' I said. 'It seems he's been wasting his time. So is he still around? I need to eliminate him from my enquiries, as they say! But he's not merely corrected our posters, even though they did contain a dodgy word—he's removed them altogether.'

'Well, all you can do is have a chat with him. His name is Algernon Flockhart. All this happened a few weeks ago, by the way, so I expect he still lives in Aidensfield. He was a little man who always travelled by bus or bicycle as he had no car. He'll be in his early seventies, I reckon, but very active and busy. I can't remember his address but it was definitely somewhere in Aidensfield.'

'I'll find him. Thanks, Alf.'

And so I rang off, completed my paperwork and checked my official copy of the electoral register for the name of Algernon Flockhart. I discovered he lived at No. 5 Abbey Terrace in Aidensfield. I would call later this morning, but first I went for a chat with Mrs Ford at Beck Cottage. A portly woman in her mid-sixties, she was a familiar figure around Aidensfield because one of her self-imposed tasks was to collect money for a variety of charities ranging from Red Cross to Poppy Day via those specializing in children, birds or animals. She was often spotted visiting houses and rattling an empty tin, or else standing in the entrance to the shop, post office, pub or churches. No one could refuse a donation!

'Mr Rhea! Good heavens, is something wrong?'

'No.' I tried to reduce her anxiety at the sight of a bobby at her door. 'No, it's just that Mrs Lambert has told me about the disappearing posters and says you saw someone removing one from the parish noticeboard in the early hours of this morning?'

'Yes, I did. Come in, Mr Rhea and I'll tell you all about it.'

Her account was brief but very clear. She told me she lived alone and unable to sleep, she had come downstairs about two o'clock that morning and had made herself a mug of cocoa. On her way back to the bedroom she had paused on her landing which was all in darkness. She looked outside because she'd noticed a movement near the parish notice-board as she was crossing from the top of her stairs towards her room. In the rather poor light of the street, she had seen a man doing something to the board and was sure he had the glass doors open—there were no locks to secure them, merely a catch to fasten them. She watched as he carefully removed the poster by extracting the drawing pins then rolled it up and pushed it into a pannier on his bike.

'He didn't simply rip it down then?'

'No, he was most careful, Mr Rhea. And he rolled up the poster instead of stuffing it into his pannier like a piece of waste paper.'

I now began to question her in more depth. 'I appreciate it was dark and a very poor light, but can you recall anything more about him? Do you know him, for example? Would you recognize him?'

'I didn't recognize him. The only thing I noticed was how small he was, almost like a young boy, and I never saw his face. He might have been wearing a cap or hat of some sort, and he was dressed all in black. Or, to be accurate, it looked black from where I was standing, certainly he wore dark clothing.'

'Did you gain any idea of his age?'

'Not really. All I remember was that he was somewhat smaller than an average man. But not a dwarf . . . about my height, Mr Rhea.'

'I'd say you were about five feet two inches tall?'

'I am, yes.'

'Right. Now you mentioned a bicycle and said it had panniers. Is there anything else about it? Was it a racing bike with dropped handlebars? Or a sedate sit-up-and-beg type?'

'I couldn't honestly tell. It didn't have lights on, though, I do remember that.'

'So he carefully rolled up a poster and pushed it into his pannier. I find it odd that he didn't throw it away or treat it as waste paper.'

'I must admit that when I first saw him, I thought he was removing an old poster, one that was out of date. They do get left behind, you know, and clutter up noticeboards once an event is over. Some become most unsightly and, I might add, very misleading. If he had been removing old notices, he would have been doing us all a service.'

'So what happened next? Did he have more posters in his panniers?'

'Not that I could see, Mr Rhea, I only noticed ours sticking out of the top.'

'So he left the top open with the tip of the poster showing?'

'Yes, then he just cycled off in the darkness with no lights. I lost him very quickly once he got into the deeper shadows. I had no idea whether he had taken any other posters, I just saw the one.'

'Thanks, Mrs Ford, this has been most helpful. I'll now make a few more enquiries and let you know the outcome in due course.'

As I left her, I felt that the man she'd seen—a small man with a bicycle—could fit Alf Ventress's brief description of Algernon Flockhart, the man with a mania for correcting spelling mistakes. So was he the sort of person who would remove any posters that offended his sensibilities? From what

Alf had said, he seemed to be exactly that sort of character. He was next on my list.

His terraced house was one of a row of six tiny cottages with no gardens and nothing to the rear except a coalshed. To get coal into that shed, the coalman had to carry it through the house, not the most welcome of intrusions. When I rapped on the door knocker, a small man answered. Sporting heavy-rimmed spectacles and with a mop of thick white hair he was in his seventies, I estimated, and wearing loose grey trousers that looked a shade too big, and a blue sweater that needed a thorough washing.

'Mr Flockhart?'

'Yes, Constable, is there a problem?'

'I'd like a word with you, if that is convenient, preferably indoors.'

'Oh, yes, of course.'

As I followed him into the house, I noticed a bicycle with panniers parked in the entrance hall; it was a gent's black cycle with upright handlebars. He led me into his tiny kitchen and pulled out a chair. I sat down.

'Can I offer you a cup of tea, Constable? Forgive me, but I rarely get visitors and I am not really prepared for callers.'

'No thanks, I've just had my breakfast. So, Mr Flockhart, this is a rather peculiar enquiry. Can I ask if you were out and about in the village late last night? With your cycle?'

'Yes, I was. I cannot deny that.'

'May I ask where you went?'

'Around the village, Constable, and to the neighbouring villages on a circular route. Well, as near as possible to a circular route.'

'And the time?'

'From just before two perhaps, only for an hour or so.'

'For exercise perhaps? To make you sleep?'

'To make me sleep, yes. I was kept awake by the incompetence of those who should know better, Constable, and so, after lying awake for a long, long time, I decided I should do something about it.'

'Go on.'

'You don't know what I am talking about, do you?'

'Could it involve the posters for St Aidan's Churchyard Fair?'

'Yes it is precisely that. Have you seen them?'

'I have indeed.'

'And did you notice anything incorrect about them?'

'I did,' I said, with a smile on my face. 'They use the word "fayre" when there is no such word.'

'Well done, Constable. That is why I could not sleep. I spent hours wondering what I could or should do about it.'

'So you went out on your bike and took down all the offending posters. Or as many as you could find.'

'I did. I am not ashamed to admit it.'

'So what have you done with them? I hope you haven't destroyed them . . .'

'I am not so stupid, Constable. Come with me.'

He led me up his narrow stairs to a back bedroom that had been converted into a study and there were the posters, all in one large pile on one side of his desk.

'I was late home. I slept late this morning and breakfasted late, but now I can get to work. I have some large white sticky labels, all blank, and I shall stick one over the word "fayre" every time it appears, and write the correct word on it. I am going to amend all those posters, and then I shall replace them well ahead of the time of the fair. I removed them secretly because I felt sure someone would object if they saw what I was doing, but they won't object if they see me putting them back in broad daylight.'

'Some of the organizers are rather upset about this, Mr Flockhart. The posters need to be in position to gain the maximum benefit for as long as possible. We need people to read them some days before the event, so they can make their plans.'

'The posters will all be back where they came from before lunch,' he promised. 'And then I shall contact the local press to gain some publicity from all this. That should put your fair on the map, eh?'

'The press?'

'Yes, the local *Evening Gazette*. It comes out on Tuesday so I am sure we can generate a lot of publicity through this. The fair will receive its share, and my campaign will too.'

And he smiled at the success of his mission. I thanked him for his openness and left. He had not committed any offence of which I was aware and if he could generate some press publicity for our fair, then it would make amends for his actions. I went to tell Mrs Lambert and she seemed to accept his explanation even if his tactics were unorthodox, but when the posters reappeared later that day, they all bore the legend 'Fayre's Fair.'

There was a press article in the *Gazette* on the Tuesday before the event and bore the headlines, FAYRE'S FAIR with details of our forthcoming event and a quote from Mr Flockhart saying how he had amended the word 'fayre'. We could not have asked for more publicity and so the church-yard fair became known as St Aiden's Churchyard Fayre's Fair.

We attracted a large crowd on a very warm and sunny day. Our efforts raised £1,235 for the church roof fund, but we now had a headline we could use whenever we wanted further publicity.

'Fayre's fair, Constable,' smiled Mr Flockhart, when I saw him hurling some white balls at a coconut shy.

'Fair enough,' was all I could think of replying.

8. FAIR OF FACE

There is an old verse that goes:

Monday's child is fair of face,
Tuesday's child is full of grace,
Wednesday's child is full of woe,
Thursday's child has far to go,
Friday's child is loving and giving,
Saturday's child works hard for a living.
But the child that is born on the Sabbath Day
Is bonny and blithe and good and gay.

I should point out that, in the lines of this verse, the word 'gay' means happy, carefree and charming, unlike the modern interpretation that implies homosexuality.

Charlotte Linford, a girl of seventeen or eighteen who lived in Aidensfield, had been born on a Monday, so the villagers told me, and the old rhyme certainly applied to her. She lived with her parents, Sally and Michael, in a large stone-built house near the church where her father maintained a smallholding while also working for the Rural District Council. His job was at their offices in Ashfordly to which he drove each morning where he worked in the

Engineers and Surveyors Department. There were two other girls in the family, Sarah and Elizabeth, both younger than Charlotte and currently at secondary school.

They went off by bus each morning and were certainly very attractive children, but they lacked the all-round charisma of their big sister. By any standards Charlotte was one of the most beautiful young women in the district. Slightly taller than average with a naturally sensuous style of walking, she had a lovely face, a slender but well-proportioned figure, nice legs, a warm personality and in addition to all those assets, she oozed oceans of charm. She was modest too and never considered herself any better than other girls. I don't think she tried to conceal her beauty but certainly did not flaunt it; I think she did not fully appreciate her own impact upon others, especially the male of the species. That famous walk of hers was totally natural and not the product of any desire to impress. Her delightful face had the benefit of lovely blue eyes and was crowned by a head of blonde hair that she wore in a variety of styles. Truly she was a picture and no matter what clothes she wore or whatever her hairstyle of the day, her beauty always shone through. She was one of those young women who could always appear glamorous whether dressed in a sack or in a motor mechanic's oil-covered overalls. Even if she had been caught in a sudden thunderous downpour that resulted in bedraggled hair and soaked clothing, she would make anyone else look like a drowned rat. Whatever the circumstances, therefore, Charlotte would emerge as a photogenic beauty. It was not surprising that some thought she could have a successful career as a fashion model, but that did not seem to interest her.

She was quite content to spend her life in and around her beloved village. The Linfords had lived in Aidensfield for centuries and Charlotte's house had been the home of her grandparents and even her great-grandparents. Aidensfield had a long and happy relationship with the Linfords.

As a young Catholic child Charlotte had attended the local primary school and then St Hilda's Convent Grammar

School in Eltering where she had shown a high degree of devotion with a deep respect for her faith. She had no wish to advance to a university education and there was even a suggestion that she might become a nun. She did not go ahead with that idea, and when I arrived in Aidensfield she was working behind the counter of Boots The Chemists at Eltering. The manager, Eddie Harrison, had the wisdom to associate her with the company's nationwide beauty products so that she sold everything from lipstick to hair shampoo by way of make-up, perfume and nail varnish. Her counter also sold inexpensive middle-of-the-range jewellery such as ear-rings, brooches, rings, bracelets and necklaces. Indeed, one of Charlotte's practices was to wear lots of bracelets on her right wrist with her watch on her left, and she favoured fashionable dangling ear-rings in a range of colours. Charlotte was good at her job and had a natural talent for advising other women about their beauty care, some much older than she. She was a walking advertisement for her products.

Charlotte travelled to work by bus—not the school bus. Every day except Sunday she went from Aidensfield to Eltering, a journey of about forty minutes. To catch her bus she would stride out from her parents' home to the bus stop, a walk of about ten minutes. It took her along the length of the main street to Aidensfield's solitary bus stop. She caught the 8.10 a.m. bus from outside Aidensfield Stores to arrive at Eltering in time for work at 9 a.m. Afterwards, she would catch the 5.15 p.m. bus from Eltering to arrive back in Aidensfield just before six o'clock. She had Wednesday afternoons off because it was half-day closing and sometimes went to visit friends in Eltering or even Scarborough because there was little to occupy her back home in Aidensfield. She worked a full day on a Saturday, but Sundays were always free because the shop was closed. Sometimes she would remain in Eltering after work to go to the cinema or to a pop concert in Scarborough and perhaps out for a drink with some of her work mates, then she would catch the 10 p.m. bus back to Aidensfield.

Because Charlotte was so pretty, most of the men in Aidensfield, old and young, were aware of her daily routine. Quite a lot of them, particularly unmarried or unattached young men would contrive to be somewhere on her route at the time she passed by. Her daily trek to catch the bus meant she had little time to pause *en route* for casual chatter, but I think those fellows wanted the opportunity merely to say 'Hello' or perhaps simply to catch the tiniest of glimpses of her. It was clear that many lived in the hope she might notice them, always with the chance of becoming more closely acquainted with her.

As she went about the start of her daily routine, there-fore, some men and youths walked their dogs, others wheeled their bikes, or found reason to pump up their bicycle tyres and went to post a letter at the time of day she was expected to pass by. Yet more paid early visits to the village shop, ostensibly to buy a newspaper or crisps and drinks for their mid-morning breaks. Fortuitously, the Aidensfield Stores opened at 7 a.m. because it sold newspapers and magazines, but village males who were smitten with Charlotte went in to buy things they didn't really need. It was all done in the hope of catching her eye and attracting her attention. Lots of admiring youngsters bought gallons of lemonade and bagsful of chocolate bars while she was heading for the bus stop. It was said that some lads caught the bus to Eltering sim-ply to be aboard at the same time as she, and then caught the next one back home. But none of them approached her. Being country-bred lads, I think they were too shy to present themselves to Charlotte as suitors—after all, a beautiful girl like that would have dozens of sophisticated admirers, prob-ably in Eltering, so the lads of Aidensfield seemed content to adore her from a distance. I learned later that on the few occasions she was approached for a date or even a walk into the woods, she would smile and say, 'Sorry, I'm engaged.' Few tried to make a date once she uttered those words and news of her engagement spread rapidly among her admirers to keep them at bay. Conventions of that time meant that decent fellows did not try to woo an engaged girl—one who was 'spoken for'—but of course they could still admire her from a distance. I had noticed the effect she had upon lusty young lads during my patrols around the village but as the new constable, it would take me a while to learn their names. However, I did notice one in particular, probably because I had seen him at mass.

He was always smartly dressed and drove a small red sports car that he parked outside the shop while buying his *Daily Mail* and some pies for lunch. It was evident to me that he timed his visit to coincide with Charlotte's arrival to catch her bus. Every time I saw Charlotte walking to the bus stop, that young man would be sitting alone in his car; if the day was fine and sunny, the top would be open; if it was raining or cold, he would sit there with the top closed but his driver's window open. One day, I asked Jack Carver, the shop owner, if he knew who the lad was.

'He's called Mark, Mr Rhea. Mark Britten. A really nice lad but one of the shyest on earth. I reckon he comes here every morning just to watch young Charlotte get onto the bus, or hoping to catch a smile from her. He's not alone, you might have noticed there are others around too, but like most of the others he's too backward—or perhaps too shy—to approach her. She's engaged anyway, or so she tells everyone. That's put a damper on things and it keeps the wolves at bay. Mark's only twenty but he's a real decent sort and he's found a good job at Ashfordly Printing Works.'

'Faint heart ne'er won fair lady?' I couldn't think of anything else to add.

'Well, if he wants her, he'll have to buck up his ideas. I'm not sure who she's supposed to be engaged to because I've never seen her with anyone. I reckon it's just a dodge to stop fellows pestering her, but he shouldn't let that put him off chatting her up. I think she's too young to be engaged—as I said, I reckon it's nothing but a pretence to stop certain men pestering her. One of these fine days, though, somebody's going to win her over although to be honest she doesn't pay much attention to the local lads. If she is engaged, it could be somebody who works away, like a sailor or a serviceman. Actually, pretending to be engaged isn't a bad idea. With her looks, she's bound to be pestered by a load of no-hopers.'

Whether Charlotte was aware of all her admirers and their tactics is not known and there is no doubt she was considered rather cold towards boys. However, she was polite enough to acknowledge anyone who smiled or spoke to her, even if it was nothing more than 'Hello' or just a smile in return, but she never encouraged them to make any further contact and for some, that small acknowledgement was ample reward for their efforts.

Charlotte was no longer a child so one might have expected some light banter between her and her admirers, but, of course, due to my fairly recent arrival, I had never known her during her school days. She might have been completely different when growing up. I did wonder whether she had once had an unpleasant experience with a man or youth? That was quite possible.

As the village constable, I was aware of, and amused by, all this very persistent and open male fascination with her, but one thing struck me as somewhat unusual especially as some believed she was engaged. As I saw her walking along the village street either coming or going from work, or merely enjoying a stroll, I had never seen her with a boyfriend. Surely, if she were engaged he would have visited her at home? Jack Carver had hinted that her engagement story might be a ploy to keep unwelcome admirers at a distance, or that her beau might be away from home in the armed forces. I reasoned that if she had ever walked out with a boy, she must have kept it a very closely guarded secret and if she did have a fiancé he was certainly keeping his distance. I thought it was all rather odd. It was almost certain she did not have a boyfriend in Aidensfield nor indeed one who visited the village to court her. I began to wonder whether she had male friends whom she'd met through work. Someone special in Eltering perhaps? Is that where her fiancé lived and worked?

Although she served on what was essentially a shop counter for women and girls, I felt sure she would have attracted the interest of some lads in Eltering.

But even if her fiancé lived in and around Eltering, he would surely be a regular visitor to Aidensfield, even visiting her at home. I knew her parents sufficiently well to know they would welcome any friend of hers into their house. If a suitor did not have his own transport, as indeed was the case with many young men, a determined Romeo or betrothed would surely find a way to reach her in Aidensfield. After all, there was a good bus service and hitch-hiking could often pay dividends.

Another interesting aspect of her life was that she did not appear to have formed a friendship with any local girls of her age. Girls tended to go out together especially if they ventured into town to visit the cinema or go to a dance, but not Charlotte. Despite her charm and her stunning appearance, it seemed she was very much a loner. As a Catholic myself, I wondered if this had anything to do with her convent education and her deep faith. Was she still contemplating being a nun? Could she have been warned about becoming very closely involved with a young man at too early an age?

Not surprisingly, I began to puzzle about Charlotte—it could be argued that her lifestyle was no concern of mine, but it is important that village constables know everything that is happening on their beats. Such awareness is known as local knowledge, something acquired only through long observation and amplified with a detailed analysis of events. A knowledge and understanding of everything and everyone has always been beneficial to the work of a rural bobby and information of that kind could often lead to the solution of minor crimes and the settlement of local disputes.

As the weeks and months went by, I realized Charlotte did not frequent the pub like others of her age and, so far as I knew, she did not visit the local tourist hotspots or nearby towns for an exciting night-life. The only exceptions were occasional nights out with colleagues from work if there was a celebration of some kind, such as a birthday, and none of those parties was held in Aidensfield. That did sound like the behaviour of someone who was engaged to be married. To add to the enigma that was Charlotte, I never saw her participating in any sport—there was a thriving tennis club in the village—neither did she attend evening classes.

Most of the time, she seemed to come from work then rarely venture outside her home, apart from those few occasions she returned from Eltering or Scarborough on a late bus. I do not know whether she ever stayed the night or a weekend at a friend's house in Eltering or elsewhere, neither did I know whether boys had ever accompanied her, or any of her friends, on those outings. She attended mass every Sunday though and on Holy Days, and took an active part in church matters such as singing in the choir and helping at social events.

It all meant that the lovely Charlotte was something of a mystery to me and so I felt sure she must be a mystery to others.

Then, one evening around seven o'clock after I had finished my tour of duty, someone knocked on the door. I answered it to find Charlotte standing there.

'Oh, Charlotte. Hello, come in.'

I knew her well enough to address her by her first name as we attended the same church and had met on several occasions. I led her into my office and settled her on the chair near my desk as I took the other seat. As she settled down, she was saying, 'I hope I'm not a nuisance, Mr Rhea, but I'm not long home from work so I couldn't come earlier.'

'It's no problem,' I assured her. 'So how can I help?'

'Do the police deal with lost property? It's just that a friend at work said you did, so I thought I'd call to see you but I wondered if it was only stolen property that you dealt with.'

'We do a lot of work involving lost and found property; in fact we have special registers for it. So, have you lost something? Or found something?'

'I've lost something.' She showed me her wrist bearing its varied collection of bracelets and bangles. 'It's one of my bracelets.' It was then that I noticed none of her fingers bore a ring—so was she really engaged?

'Do you think it is lost, or could it have been stolen?' I had to ask the question because if it had been stolen, I would have to compile a crime report and launch a modest investigation.

'Oh, I'm sure I've lost it; it couldn't have been stolen from my wrist.' She nodded her pretty head fiercely. 'It is quite old and I think the chain was rather worn. If it fell off my wrist I might not have noticed it was missing, it was always among all the others.'

'OK.' I retrieved my own lost property register from under my desk and opened it on the desktop. 'Where do you think you lost it?'

'I'm not sure,' she admitted. 'And I don't know when I lost it either. You can see I wear a lot of them together. I take them all off at night so if one has fallen off, I really can't say where or when that was. But it was today at work when I discovered it was missing.'

'Could it have been on the bus to work?'

'Yes, I suppose it could. I spoke to the conductor on the home bus tonight and she said she would record it; they have a lost and found property office at their Scarborough depot. If it is there, she will get in touch with me. She's often on the bus I use for work.'

'Fine. But if it was lost in the street we can deal with it. Could it have been lost here in Aidensfield or in Eltering?'

'I suppose it could be in either place but I can't be sure. I have looked around the shop where I work but it's not there, and I have alerted the cleaner. If she finds it, she'll let me know.'

'Good, we're not unduly concerned with property lost or found in private premises, so you've done all the right things. So we need to concentrate either here in Aidensfield or somewhere in Eltering.'

175

She nodded. 'I can't think where else it could be. It's not at home, by the way, I've checked and Mum looked around all the rooms before I came to tell you.'

'Right, well, I'll take a description with as much detail as possible.'

'Thank you, Mr Rhea, I do hope it turns up.'

'We'll do our best to trace it. We don't make a special search for such things but, obviously, I will keep my ears and eyes open around the village and would suggest you do the same.'

'I've already searched around the village but didn't find it.'

'It might need more than one very thorough search and let me know if you do find it. Meanwhile I'll check the found property registers at both Ashfordly and Eltering police stations. If it has been found and handed in to the police, we'll know about it, and we'll contact you.'

'Thank you.'

'Now, if it is found, would you be able to recognize it as yours? From my limited knowledge, there are lots of bracelets that look very much like each other.'

'Oh, yes, but I would recognize this one, Mr Rhea. It's got my initials CL scratched inside, along with JB, that's Joseph Britten. And there is a heart between, with an arrow through the heart.' As she spoke I recalled the surname of the lad in the sports car always parked outside the shop as she was catching her bus—it was also Britten, but Mark, not Joseph.

'Your boyfriend?' I asked, then realized it was a rather intrusive question. So perhaps she was unofficially engaged?

She blushed and nodded, saying, 'Yes, Joseph wouldn't want me to lose it. It means such a lot to both of us.'

'Of course, so the bracelet has great sentimental value?'

She nodded.

'Right, then tell me what it looks like.'

She described it as being a band of metal that was coloured silver, but she didn't think it was actually made of silver. In her opinion, it was a metal of some kind that could be polished to make it shine. The width of the metal used to make the band was about quarter of an inch (6mm). It was thin, less than a sixteenth of an inch thick (1mm or so) and it could be bent quite easily by one's fingers. For that reason, the bracelet was not a perfect circle or a perfect oval—it was slightly misshapen through fair wear and tear. It also had a catch which could be adjusted to cater for wrists of varying sizes. There was no security chain if the catch became loose or got broken.

'It wasn't a very expensive one, in fact it was very cheap,' she volunteered when I asked about the security chain. 'I think only the better quality ones have those little chains.'

'But expensive ones also get lost! So it wasn't one of those fashionable charm bracelets?'

'Oh no, it was very plain and simple with no trimmings.'

Having obtained as detailed a description as possible, I realized the critical information, from an identification point of view, were those sets of initials and the heart carved or scratched inside the bracelet.

'So what is it worth?' was my next question. 'Can you put a value on it?'

'Moneywise, it's almost nothing, Mr Rhea; it's the sort of thing you might find at a jumble sale, or even as a prize in a fairground machine.'

'I need to show a value in our records, just to prove it's not really a silver or gold item that's been lost. Shall we say ten shillings?'

'More like one shilling!' she smiled. 'Really, it's not worth anything, Mr Rhea, probably only a few pence. It's just that I've had it for a long time and hate the fact I might never see it again. I'll ask my mum and dad to help, then I'll have another look for it in the street and around the village, as you suggest.'

Before she left my office, I rang the duty constables at both Eltering and Ashfordly Police Stations but neither had received any report of the finding of the bracelet. Both took down its description and entered it in their own records—I would be informed if it was reported found at either of those stations.

'It's not been handed in, Charlotte and, as I promised, I'll do my bit even though we don't normally search for lost property. I'll ask at the post office, shop and pubs, just to see if anyone's handed it in there. That happens sometimes.'

'Thank you.'

'And don't forget that if it does turn up, please let me know.'

'Yes I will, I promise.'

And so Charlotte Linford left and my office suddenly seemed dull, uninspiring and bare. It was amazing the effect a pretty girl can have upon a fellow! There was never any real urgency about circulating descriptions of lost property unless it was something hazardous like drugs, explosives or even dangerous animals, although we would always try to alert the public to losses of very valuable or important items. There is the oft-told story about a caravanner who pulled into a filling station to top up his fuel tank. At the time, his mother-in-law was asleep in the caravan he was towing, but when it stopped she thought they had reached their destination. Realizing the caravan was stationary and empty, she got out.

Meanwhile, the driver had returned to his car and, not noticing mother-in-law standing behind the unit, drove off. She was left stranded on the forecourt while he rejoined the holiday traffic and disappeared. She had no idea where she was, neither did she know the registration number of his car; furthermore, he had no idea she'd been left behind at a filling station the location of which he did not know. Losing one's mother-in-law is probably one of those instances where a public appeal via the radio and newspapers is a good idea and I believe they were eventually reunited through such publicity.

I recalled another instance where a bus driver lost his bus and its complement of forty-five passengers. He had parked it in a busy seaside car park, one of many in the resort, and had then forgotten which one it was. He couldn't find his way back. At the appointed time, his passengers returned and sat there waiting for their driver; in the meantime, he had decided to inform the police that he had lost his bus. We found it eventually but not until the park in question had almost emptied.

Charlotte's loss was not the kind of problem that would attract publicity unless the bracelet was the subject of a very strong and emotive story. Besides, its absence could be traced to a fairly small location—one possibility was Charlotte's walk from home to the bus stop, and the other was her route from the bus to her place of work in Eltering. In either case, of course, someone could have picked up the bracelet and recognizing its low value, could have thrown it away never to be seen again.

Next morning I undertook a foot patrol around Aidensfield specifically to try and find Charlotte's bracelet because it meant so much to her. Although hunting for lost property is not part of a police officer's duty, there are times one must use a bit of common sense and exercise a modicum of community spirit. I would not tell Sergeant Blaketon of my search, and if he asked what I was doing, I would merely tell him I was patrolling Aidensfield to keep the peace and prevent crime. As I walked around the village therefore, I kept my eyes peeled for any sign of such a trinket on the road or footpath while bearing in mind it could have been kicked into the gutter or thrown onto the grass.

My first call was the village shop. Due to its secondary business as the local newsagent and the post office it was always busy and that morning was no exception. I walked in and decided to announce my quest to everyone, not just to Jack and Jill Carver, the owners.

Mark Britten's sports car was parked outside, empty, and when I entered I noticed he was in the queue waiting to pay for his purchases.

'Morning everyone,' I boomed above the chatter. 'There's a small matter I'd like you all to think about.'

They lapsed into silence as I told them about the lost bracelet without revealing the identity of its owner. I referred to the initials scratched inside, however, so perhaps a bright person might draw some conclusions from that, but I asked that if anyone found it lying in the street or elsewhere, they should return it to me and I would restore it to its owner. I stressed its emotional value and repeated the same exercise in the Brewers' Arms, the garage and the surgery. But no one had found it and everyone promised to keep their eyes open in the hope they would locate it. If it didn't turn up, I would consider placing a printed poster on the noticeboards in those establishments and also on my police noticeboard—I might suggest that idea to Charlotte. I was sure her father could produce a suitable advertisement after his experiences of working for the Rural District Council.

That morning, Charlotte boarded her bus as usual and I watched it pull away, with Mark Britten then leaving the scene to head off to Ashfordly. I noticed he had not spoken to Charlotte. The other men and lads made their way either back home to their farms, smallholdings or home-based places of work, or else they disappeared either to Ashfordly and Eltering for their jobs. The area became suddenly very quiet.

At home, and indeed during my tours of duty in the days that followed, I thought about Charlotte's loss but did not make any enquiries about her love life. However, despite my efforts and those of Charlotte and her family along with help from some of the villagers, the bracelet was not found. One man even turned up with a metal detector and he scoured the paths and roads in the village and although he found a good deal of useless junk, along with a florin, a few shillings, pennies and a horseshoe, he did not find Charlotte's bracelet. And so the matter rested.

A few days after she had reported her loss, I made a point of being near the bus stop as she waited for her bus to work. I noticed the usual crowd of lads and men ostensibly busy at the shop, and Mark Britten sitting in his usual place in his car. Nothing had changed. I managed to hail Charlotte to ask whether she had found her bracelet at work or in Eltering, but her answer was a shake of that pretty head. I told her of my actions but said I had not found it either.

'Thanks for all you've done,' she said, as the bus driver prepared to pull away. 'I doubt if it will be found now. Maybe I shall have to accept that it has gone for ever.'

'We'll all keep looking,' I called, as she was carried away from us. I watched Mark Britten drive away too, not speeding away with a hefty roar of the engine as some young men might have done in their sports cars, but gliding peacefully down the road as he went off to work.

At that stage, I thought the mini-saga of the lost bracelet was over, but it wasn't. A week or two later, the annual Bartholomew Fair was held on St Aidan's Field to celebrate St Bartholomew's feast day. The feast day, which fell on 24 August, had been celebrated for centuries in Aidensfield because it marked the safe gathering of the harvest and was sometimes known by its ancient name of Bartle Fair. Bartle Fairs were held in many other towns and villages throughout England, one of the biggest being at Smithfield in London. This one had started in 1133 and it continued until 1752, the year Pope Gregory's new calendar was brought into effect in England after almost two centuries of resistance. One famous Bartle Fair continues at West Witton in Wensleydale, North Yorkshire and is known as the Witton Feast. An effigy of Old Bartle is still ceremoniously burnt—it was reckoned that this particular Bartle was a notorious cattle thief.

I was scheduled for duty at the fair because it always attracted a large crowd. This was before the revival of St Aidan's Churchyard Fair so, in the future, there would be a clash of interests. One day at some time in the future, both fairs would be amalgamated.

However, the day in question was hot with a cloudless sky and blazing sunshine. The usual range of stalls and attractions were spread around the field, along with a marquee hosting a buffet lunch and a bar. Many of the local people had taken a day off work to attend, and, of course, the nearby schools were closed for their summer holidays. It meant the children had a splendid day's entertainment with everything from a Punch and Judy show to the mock-up of a small beach with sand and water, courtesy of a local builder. Mary came along with our children as the fair came to life, buzzing with sounds of laughter and happiness.

There was very little for me to do except to patrol the grounds in my uniform, although I did guide one or two bruised children and their mums to the first aid tent, and others to the lost children's tent. As the heat of the day began to take its toll, I found a shady place in the shadows of the refreshment marquee. I was alone in my effort to cool down and Mary brought me an ice cream. She left me as she went off to see to the children who were playing in the sand with some friends.

As I welcomed the coolness of the ice cream, I saw Mark Britten heading towards me. Dressed in a short-sleeved shirt and shorts, he seemed somewhat shy about approaching me, so I smiled and said, 'Hello, Mark. Are you looking for me?'

'Yes, I am, Mr Rhea. Sorry if I've come at an awkward time . . .' and he looked at my ice cream as it rapidly melted in the hot sun. 'But I saw you come around here where it's quiet and I wanted a chat, just you and me.'

'Well, here I am, so if you don't mind me cooling down with this . . . I've nearly finished it!'

'No, of course not.'

'So what can I do for you?' I spoke as the melting cream ran down the side of the remaining section of cornet with most of it being caught in the base. I decided I must finish it and so completed the task in one large bite, cornet and all.

'It's about that bracelet that Charlotte Linford lost,' he said quietly. 'I've found it.'

He dug into his pocket and pulled out the trinket, passing it to me. I turned it over to try and find the inscription. Then I saw it. It was not really an inscription but a crudely scratched set of initials with a pair of letters at each side of a heart pierced with an arrow. It was obviously Charlotte's piece of lost property and it appeared to me that the marks had probably been scratched with the point of a sharp knife or something similar. In my view, it looked like the work of a child and indeed the bracelet was hardly the sort a grown woman would wear. It was too cheap and very childish—little wonder she had concealed it among her others.

'This looks like the one, Mark. Well done. Charlotte will be pleased.'

'I found it in the rough grass at the side of the path that Charlotte uses when she walks to the bus,' he explained. 'I've had it for a few days but, well, I know it's silly, but I don't like to approach her with it . . . I thought of taking it to her house but, well, I couldn't pluck up the courage. I didn't know what her parents might think.'

'I'm not sure I understand your caution . . . but she's not here today.'

'No, I've got the day off work. I thought she might be here, but I saw her get on the bus to go to work this morning as usual. It's not that I'm shy . . . I am, but this is a bit complicated. I don't know how much you know about Charlotte and that bracelet . . .'

'Not a lot,' I admitted. 'She told me she'd lost it and provided a good description. She did tell me about the inscription, saying it was her initials and those of a boyfriend called Joseph Britten. That's all she said and although I've heard she is engaged, I must admit I've never seen her with a boyfriend, nor do I know Joseph Britten.'

'No you wouldn't, Mr Rhea, it was a long time ago.'

'Oh.' And now I sensed some kind of drama of which I was not aware. 'So is there something more to this than meets the eye? She told me her boyfriend was called Joseph Britten—is he related to you?'

'Yes.' He paused. 'Yes, he's my cousin.'

'Right, but I've not come across him in the village.'

'No, you wouldn't—he lives in Australia. His mum and dad went out there about eight years ago, to make a better life for themselves. All their children went with them—Joseph has three brothers and a sister, they're all living near Brisbane and doing well, so I am told. We keep in touch, if only at Christmas!'

'So you mean Charlotte hasn't seen him since then?'

He nodded. 'It's a bit sad really, Mr Rhea. Look, am I holding you up? I didn't know whether I should bother you with this, but when I found the bracelet I knew it belonged to Charlotte—when we were kids Joe told me he'd given it to her. We were close, me and him, we're cousins as I said, but we were play-mates as well, and the best of pals.'

'That sounds a bit like my young days, some of my cousins were my best friends. In a small village, there's often no one else. So you haven't told Charlotte you've found her bracelet?'

'No, not yet. I was waiting for a chance to give it to her after I'd found it but chickened out because of what it means to her. I heard you tell people about it in the shop recently and then saw the notices, so I thought I'd better hand it in to you, to make it official. I wondered if you would return it to her. I daren't, you see, I couldn't bring myself to do so, but I think she should have it back.'

I sensed a mystery here. 'This all sounds mighty intriguing, Mark, and, of course, I shall be pleased to return it to her. Clearly you know more about this bracelet than I shall ever know, so can I ask why you are so reluctant to return it yourself?'

'Policemen are expected to keep secrets, aren't they?'

'Well, yes, we do encounter a lot of secrets during our work and we know when to keep our mouths shuts.'

'I thought so. Well, Mr Rhea, I can tell you, but I don't want you to tell Charlotte or her parents that I have told you this.'

'You have my word.'

'Well, it's probably nothing really, but it meant so much to Charlotte at the time. When both of them were children she went everywhere with Joseph. They were the best of friends, absolutely inseparable. Then they decided they would get married to each other—they were ten years old.'

'Ah!' I now began to sense the sentimental value of that bracelet. 'So Charlotte is waiting for him to return from Australia?'

'It's a bit more complicated than that, Mr Rhea. They actually got married.'

'Got married?'

He was smiling now and I could see his confidence growing as he related this tale.

'Well, engaged might be the better word. Or perhaps I should say they made a commitment to each other. We were all only about nine or ten years old at the time, me and them, and some other pals. During the summer holidays we went into the Catholic Church here in Aidensfield. It's always open so we borrowed some of the priest's vestments from the vestry. I got dressed up in them, so I became the priest. We had two bridesmaids and a best man, and Charlotte sneaked out in the dress she'd worn when she made her first communion, it looked just like a bride's white dress. She covered it up with a coat on the way to church. Joseph put his best suit on . . . all without our parents knowing. The bridesmaids also put on their first communion frocks and hid them under coats as we walked to the church. I think anyone who saw us would have thought we were going to a fancy dress party. Anyway, we staged a wedding in the church. It was lovely, Mr Rhea. We all took it so seriously. We said our prayers and the bride and groom exchanged their vows from an order of wedding service sheet that we found at the back of the church . . .'

'There are some who would say that was a legitimate wedding if the promises were sincere,' I smiled. 'Except that the participants were only ten so that's a bit on the young side for an English wedding!'

'We all took it very seriously, especially Charlotte. She had a very strong religious attitude, you know, and still has. However, complications started when Joseph and his family went to Australia about eight years ago, not long after that so-called wedding, so Charlotte, having made promises about parting only upon death, decided she should wait for Joseph to return. In her mind, that was the promise she had made. To wait for ever.'

'You mean she's still waiting?'

'Yes,' he said. 'She is. Eight years isn't long, especially when most of them were spent when she was a child at school. But that's why she doesn't bother with other boy-friends; she tells them she's engaged. I honestly think she still believes she is.'

'So when is Joseph expected back?' was my next question.

'He's never coming back, Mr Rhea, that's the real problem behind all this. And worse still, she doesn't know.'

'Oh crumbs,' was all I could think of saying. Then, after a pause, I asked, 'I can see why you hesitate to return it. So why isn't he coming back to England?'

'The day before I found that bracelet, my mum and dad got word that Joseph had got engaged and his wedding is going to take place in Australia some time next year. We'll all be invited—our family that is. Not Charlotte though, he's obviously forgotten her. I must admit I'd forgotten that childish wedding until all this happened.'

'Poor Charlotte. Do you honestly think she's been waiting all this time?'

'Yes, I do. She is still waiting for him, Mr Rhea, because she says she made a promise before God. So far as I know, she's had no word from Joseph in recent years. He wrote some letters after he first went out there, but nothing since he grew up. He's nineteen now . . . he's still very young but it's his life and he'll be twenty—nearly twenty-one in fact—when he gets married. His bride-to-be is Australian, by the way.'

'I can see why that bracelet is so important. We could say it has served like an engagement ring.'

'Yes, but only I know its secret and Charlotte of course. The other children who were present moved away from Aidensfield and in any case, I am sure they have all forgotten it,' said Mark. 'It's our secret now, mine and Charlotte's. Joe gave it to her during that wedding ceremony—their wedding ring, I suppose. So you can see why I can't return it to her

. . . I would break down. I'd be hopeless, too nervous, and it's going to upset her when she knows the truth. The news about Joseph has revived my memories, and then with me finding this bracelet . . .'

'Well, I can return it to her, that is not a problem,' I said. 'She need never know that I am aware of her devotion and certainly I shan't mention Joseph's current situation. For me, it would be a perfectly normal part of my duty. I'll be pleased to do it for you.'

'Thanks Mr Rhea, but I thought you should know why I am reluctant to hand it back to her. I am aware of Joseph's new life out there, and she is not. I think she might feel betrayed when she finds out. I am really sorry the way it has all worked out, sorry for her, I mean.'

I took the bracelet from him, saying, 'I'll consider this very carefully before I return it to her. Do I tell her you found it, for example? And do you think she knows about Joseph and his wedding? Could the news have leaked out?'

'I don't think so. My parents only knew a couple of days ago and haven't really talked about it. They don't have a lot to do with Charlotte's parents and, of course, none of the parents knew about the children's wedding. But really, Mr Rhea, you could simply return the bracelet without telling her you know the story behind it.'

'That's the only sensible way to deal with it,' I agreed. 'And I shall not say you found it, unless you want me to.'

'I don't think you should. If you mention me, it will revive all her memories. That's why I would like you to hand it over.'

'I understand. I'll do it like that. Thanks for telling me all this. But there is another question, Mark. For you, I mean. Do you think someone should tell Charlotte the truth so that she can get on with her own life instead of waiting hopelessly for Joseph?'

'I'm not sure . . .'

'Clearly Joseph does not regard those childhood vows very seriously. For him it was just a bit of fun.'

'It was fun for all of us, Mr Rhea, except Charlotte. She's the one who took it so seriously—and still does. She has been wearing that bracelet ever since.'

'I can see it's causing you a lot of concern, Mark. So, as I said, leave it with me for a day or two. I'll think about the best way to deal with this—I know I shouldn't get personally involved in matters of this kind, but I do feel some kind of affinity with Charlotte. I need to find the right time and right words when I restore it to her. I'll let you know how I get on.' And I pushed the bracelet into my pocket.

'Thanks, Mr Rhea.'

At home that evening after the children had gone to bed, I discussed the problem with my wife, Mary.

'I can't see that a young girl on the threshold of womanhood would take that kind of thing seriously,' she said. 'Let's face it, we all do things as a child that are serious at that time, but as we grow up we realize they were not worth worrying about. I can't believe she is still waiting for him to return.'

'Mark remembered the so-called wedding,' I reminded her. 'It must have made some impact on Joseph too. And no one's told Charlotte that Joseph is not coming back. I can understand why she's still waiting . . . surely the truth must come from Joseph in person, otherwise how can she know he no longer cares? He's found someone else and my guess is that he will have forgotten all about that childhood promise to Charlotte.'

'Yes, but that wedding was a joke, a bit of outlandish fun and games, just the sort of thing children would do. Surely Charlotte must realize that?'

Our discussion served only to increase my dilemma, one reason being that I was duty bound to return the property to her, otherwise I could be accused of stealing it. I had no right to keep it, and neither had Mark. It belonged to Charlotte. I slept on the problem and next morning resumed my patrol of Aidensfield. My shift was an early turn which meant I started at six in the morning. I decided to arrange things so that I was outside the Linfords' house in time to walk up to the bus stop with Charlotte so that we could have a quiet and very personal conversation. As she emerged, she spotted me and so I made the excuse that I happened to be passing and would accompany her to the bus.

Even before I had time to initiate a conversation, she said, 'Oh, Mr Rhea, I am so pleased you are here, what a wonderful coincidence. I wanted to have a word with you. I was thinking last night about that bracelet and you know what?'

'No?'

'I've decided I'm pleased I have lost it. I think it is an omen of some kind. I have come to the decision that it marks the parting of the ways between me and my boyfriend Joseph. They were his initials, as I think I told you. I believe God decided I should lose the bracelet and so sever my links with him—and he can go his own way too, out there in Australia. He hasn't written to me for a long, long time and so I feel much happier now that I have made my decision, or had it made for me. It's time for me to forget him. After all, we were only nine or ten or thereabouts when he gave me that bracelet with our initials inside. I bet he's forgotten all about it now he's living in Australia. Do you agree with that?'

'I think that is a very sensible, practical and brave decision, Charlotte.' But now I had to be slightly devious. 'So if the bracelet is ever found, would you want it returned to you?'

'No, I would not, Mr Rhea. If anyone found it and tried to return it to me, I would throw it into the dustbin. Its loss marks the end of an era of my life. So, if anyone brings it to you, just throw it away, you have my consent. I feel so free without it . . .'

'A very adult decision.' As we talked, I accompanied her to the bus stop and would record her decision in my official notebook. We approached the bus stop and Mark was there as usual, sitting outside the shop in his sports car with its hood down and he watched as I escorted Charlotte onto the bus. She waved goodbye as the bus moved off and so I went to talk to Mark.

189

'The deed is done,' I told him.

'So what happened, Mr Rhea?'

'She doesn't know the bracelet has been found—I didn't get the chance to tell her—but she regards its loss as the closing of a chapter in her life, Mark. She wants to start a new one. Those were her words. She has given me authority to dispose of it if it does turn up. She made it clear she doesn't want to see it again—and, so far as I am aware, she knows nothing of Joseph's romance at the other side of the world. I didn't mention it.'

'So the spell is broken?' he smiled.

'Yes, Mark, the spell is broken.'

'So I might ask her if she would like a drive out to Whitby or somewhere this weekend. Do you think I should do that? I'm not very good at asking girls out . . .'

'Mark, I think that would be a great idea. Don't hang about trying to decide, do it the moment she gets back from work—wait for her here, at this bus stop . . . tonight.'

'Yes, yes, I will. Thank you.'

I disposed of the bracelet where it would never be found. On the Sunday following, I was patrolling Aidensfield around ten o'clock on a very warm morning. Saint Aidan's congregation had turned out after mass and, as I walked, I heard a car horn sound behind me. Mark drove past very slowly with his roof open and I was pleased to see Charlotte at his side.

THE END

ALSO BY NICHOLAS RHEA

Thank you for reading this book.

If you enjoyed it please leave feedback on Amazon or Goodreads, and if there is anything we missed or you have a question about, then please get in touch. We appreciate you choosing our book.

Founded in 2014 in Shoreditch, London, we at Joffe Books pride ourselves on our history of innovative publishing. We were thrilled to be shortlisted for Independent Publisher of the Year at the British Book Awards.

www.joffebooks.com

We're very grateful to eagle-eyed readers who take the time to contact us. Please send any errors you find to corrections@joffebooks.com. We'll get them fixed ASAP.

Lightning Source UK Ltd.
Milton Keynes UK
UKHW010745220822
407644UK00002B/516